Signs Point to Yes

In This Series

Signs Point to Yes

Signs Point to Yes

Christopher Church

Published by Dagmar Miura
Los Angeles
www.dagmarmiura.com

Signs Point to Yes

This is a work of fiction. Names, characters, businesses, places, events, and incidents are either the products of the author's imagination or used in a fictitious manner. Any resemblance to actual persons, living or dead, or actual events is purely coincidental.

photo on page 242: Los Angeles Public Library

First published 2014

ISBN: 978-1-942267-00-3

Thursday

MASON KNEW HE'D MADE the right decision when he landed his first client the same day he posted his ad online. He quit his job that day, and rather than looking for another dead-end office job clacking away at a keyboard, the most logical thing, the right path, he decided, was to dedicate himself to making a living using his psychic abilities.

The day had started out routinely enough, like any other day in gossip-magazine publishing, with an actress who had fallen off a balcony in New York the night before. Mason had been tasked with her obituary. In the morning meeting, the senior editor, digging through her stack of notes, said, "Let's do something respectful and uplifting about her," meaning the newly dead actress, "and we'll use the photos of her at that awards thing, it must have been three or four years ago, when she wore the little black dress."

"Can't we use the photos from last month when she got thrown out of that nightclub?" Mason asked. "Those are much more current images."

The editor shook her head. "Why do you bother? You're just wasting our time."

Mason turned red. Wasting her time. He was wasting his own time, trying to make some actress sound like Indira Gandhi. He was sick of it, and with a surge of adrenaline he made a snap decision.

"I'm done wasting your time," he said, and stood up. "Screw you, and screw your dead actress." He got up and started toward the door. The editor sat in silence, watching him calmly. "I won't be back," he said, trying to keep his voice from quavering. "You can mail me my last check."

"This meeting isn't over," she had called after him. Maybe she thought he was bluffing and that he would come crawling back, but he had momentum now, and he wasn't going to backtrack. He hurriedly packed up a banker's box of his personal stuff, and plopped it on his friend Justine's desk.

"I just quit," he told her. "Can you hang on to this for me? And my key card, could you drop it with HR?"

Justine looked stunned. "Dude," was all she could say.

He trotted down to the street to unlock his bicycle, wound up by the excitement and exhilarated at the thought of not having to go back. I guess I'm now officially self-employed, he thought. It was far less terrifying than being unemployed. He'd daydreamed about this for months, leaving his job to do something he actually cared about, and now it was happening, ready or not. This is a positive turn of events, he told himself, focusing all his energy on the elation he felt so as not to let the shock morph into fear.

It was still early in the day, and the traffic was light enough that the cars raced past him on Sunset Boulevard. He changed gears and pedaled harder.

Career counselors always said "Do what you're good at," but the only thing he felt he had a natural talent for was psychic insight. Back in college he'd taken a class on the basics of making money as a psychic, which had led to holding séances with friends in college, reading tarot cards at parties, and trying to glean insight from friends' keys and jewelry. He'd gotten really good results—clear extrasensory information about people and the questions they asked. "Right on," he'd been told more than once. During a tarot reading he'd once picked up a strong vibe that a woman's father was going to die soon; it wasn't in the cards that she pulled, but an insight he got when talking to her during the reading. He didn't tell her that her father was going to die, of course, and he had no idea whether the man died or not. But the insight, the vision, had been strong, and it convinced him that, yes, he had the power.

As his job gradually became more draining, he'd thought about how to turn the power into a career. He'd kick-started the process for himself today, he realized. He took a deep breath and swung his bike onto his street, standing on the pedals to power up the hill.

He'd decided that his business model was not going to be some flimflam storefront crystal ball business, but rather, as he presented it to Ned, his boyfriend, when he got home, "a serious, professional investigator who uses psychic power to help people, to make the world a better place." He'd rehearsed that in his head on the way up the hill, and he spoke the words calmly, with a smile that he thought showed self-confidence.

"Mason, what the fuck? That was a good job. How do you plan to pay the rent?" Ned waved his arm around at their house. He wasn't a big guy, but his anger hit Mason like a sucker punch.

"Don't yell at me."

"I have to. You're acting crazy," Ned said.

"It's not crazy," Mason said. "I actually think it'll be profitable. Although it might take a while to get a consistent revenue stream going, I'll admit that."

"Revenue stream? You're going to make us homeless, is what you're going to do." Ned sat on the sofa at the side of the living room, and ran his fingers through his black hair.

"It's always about you." Mason was angry now too, and felt his cheeks redden. It was impossible to hide, as a redhead; his face immediately displayed any strong feeling. He had always thought that the stereotype of redheads being hotheaded was just that: pale skin showed things that wouldn't have been obvious in darker people. He folded his arms and didn't sit down; that way it would be easier to bolt if the conversation overheated.

"What are you talking about?" Ned said.

"Your ego, man. That thing in AA about putting aside your ego is in there because alcoholics are selfish. That's what I'm hearing right now, how my decisions impact you. Why can't you be happy for me?"

"OK, first, fuck you for bringing my sobriety into this when it's your own screwup. I've been sober for a lot longer than I've known you. And second, it is about me as much as it's about you. If you don't have a job, I'm going to have to carry you."

"This is not a screwup," Mason snapped. "I've been thinking about making a change for a while now; you know that."

"I thought you meant you were going to find another journalism job. But a psychic? You never said that. It's not even something real."

"You can be a total ass, you know that?" Mason shouted. He walked down the hall and shut himself in their bedroom, flopping down on the bed. It wasn't the right way to deal, but it was easy and familiar.

Ned left him alone. If he thought it wasn't "real," how would he ever get on board with the new plan? Maybe Mason should have given him some warning, but he was tired of being inert, and blowing up at his boss had felt like the right thing to do in the moment. He was being proactive for a change, instead of reactive; that was the way he wanted to be able to deal with the world. But maybe quitting without any notice and burning that bridge was just a reaction too.

A WHILE LATER NED knocked softly and pushed open the bedroom door. "Come out and talk to me," he said, seeming calm. His emotions flashed to the surface at lightning speed, but they tended to dissipate just as quickly. How could he just switch it off? Mason had once commented that everyone in Ned's family was like that; Ned defended it as part of their Latino culture. Mason wasn't sure if it really was a cultural thing, but even after three years he was still learning how to deal with it.

Mason followed him back to the living room. Ned sat on the sofa, but rather than sitting beside him, Mason sat on the other wing, facing him. Ned seemed contrite, but Mason wasn't quite ready for it to blow over.

"You know why I'm a bit freaked out about all this, right?" Ned asked.

"You're worried about money. Well, I'm already worried about it, so you can leave that to me."

"It's more than that," Ned said. "You've said you weren't happy at work, but you hadn't really talked about leaving your job, so it's kind of unexpected. People don't usually make such rash decisions about something so important. And don't take this the wrong way, but I think psychic power is fictional."

"Yeah, that's the second time you've said that," Mason said, irritated. "And don't take this the wrong way, but I don't really care whether you believe it or not. You can be supportive of me, regardless of whether you believe in psychic power."

"OK, Mason, I get it. You're still upset."

"I was actually feeling happy and liberated until I got home and you started freaking out. I was feeling good about finally taking charge of my own destiny."

"Well, none of that good stuff has to change just because I'm worried. I might have a big ego, but you're being too sensitive."

Mason thought for a moment and then laughed. "Like a delicate little flower."

"I was thinking more like a house of cards, but the flower image works too. Hey." Mason looked up at him, and Ned held his eyes, softer now. "I'm sorry I yelled at you."

"I'll get over it. I just need some time. English blood comes to a boil slowly, remember? It takes longer to cool down."

"Fair enough," Ned said. He rubbed his eyes, and Mason realized he looked tired. Seeing the impact the day was having on him, Mason felt a twinge of guilt.

"So can we talk about the psychic investigator thing objectively for a minute?" Ned said.

"You're starting from a place of skepticism, so no, I don't think you can be objective about it."

"Well, then, can I tell you how I feel? Calmly, this time."

"If it'll make you feel better, knock yourself out."

"OK, first off, I don't remember you ever demonstrating any psychic abilities," Ned said.

"I do psychic stuff all the time; I just don't talk about it with you because you're such a skeptic."

"Well, we're talking about it now. What evidence do you have of your psychic powers?"

"It's very subtle," Mason said, scrambling to think of an actual example.

"Uh-huh," Ned said, sounding thoroughly unconvinced.

"Remember that séance we did with Peggy and Gilbert that time?"

"Yes, but nothing really happened. The pointer just went around and around the Ouija board in random circles. It was like listening to my *abuelo* talk about politics."

"Gilbert thought it was real."

"Gilbert also thinks the pope was replaced by a cyborg controlled by the Chinese military. Which doesn't make him a great reference for your résumé."

"Don't worry. I have plenty of tools to pierce the veil of the mystic world," Mason said, and attempted a disarming grin.

Ned laughed. "Well, I hope that includes a cosmic ATM."

"I have some money set aside. I'm not going to make us homeless. It might take a little time, but I know I can make this psychic thing work. If it doesn't, I can always go back to working for the man."

"You were working for a woman at that place," Ned said, and sighed. "Have you at least looked into what you have to do to get licensed?" He leaned forward and picked up his tablet from the coffee table.

"Who licenses psychics? I'm thinking I'll be more like a freelancer, or a subcontractor."

"*I'm* thinking you'll need a private investigator's license, if you're going to investigate things."

The truth was that Mason didn't know exactly how he was going to make a living as a psychic investigator until he actually did the work, figured it out, made it happen. That was how his mind worked. Ned was the problem-solver type, and he obviously wanted to hear something more concrete right now, a step-by-step plan.

"Here," Ned said, peering at his screen. "They're licensed by the state. You have to have three years' experience in law enforcement or security work. Plus it says there's a firearms requirement." He looked up at Mason. "You're not exactly the firearms type."

"Hey, Tintin never needed a gun."

"Tintin didn't try to make a living from psychic power."

"Sweetie," Mason said, as calmly as he could, "I don't really want to be that kind of investigator. I'm thinking more about helping people with things that don't involve … weapons." He moved closer to Ned, taking his hand. From the sofa he could see just a tiny corner of the Silver Lake reservoir, glinting in the afternoon sun. "You get to be in this beautiful place all day long, enjoying the sun and the view, setting your own work hours. Look at you, you're sitting here in shorts, and you're at work. I'd love to be working that way."

"OK," Ned said, and forced a smile, but pulled his hand away. "Let's see what happens."

"And let's not overthink it," Mason said. "It's just a job transition, not a calamity. It's time for me to do this, to start taking action and do something more rewarding."

Mason was surprised to hear the words "taking action" coming out of his own mouth. That wasn't how his life usually went. He wasn't one of those mystifying people who went out boldly into the world each day, setting up businesses, moving across the country, living fearlessly. Instead, fear had been his great motivator, keeping him in situations that were comfortable rather than happy. This time, though, he felt he had some say in the direction the change would take him, and the feeling of power it gave him was even stronger than the fear.

"So all this happened over an actress who was mostly famous for misbehaving at nightclubs," Ned said, "and her swan dive from the forty-seventh floor."

"See, even you know way too much about her. Think of the amazing things that could be accumulating inside your head if it wasn't full of pointless information like that. Personally, I'm done. I don't want to know any of it anymore."

"Fair enough. Maybe if I stop reading your company's website, I'll be able to learn Tagalog or neurosurgery or something."

"My former company," Mason corrected him.

"Right. So … do I dare ask what your plan for this new venture is?"

Mason knew that if he told Ned the first step in his plan—putting an ad on Craigslist—it would only alarm him. Instead he said, "I've only been at this full-time now for, like, a couple of hours. Give me a minute to shift gears. For now I've got some computer work to do. I'll tell you more later."

Mason walked down the hall to the office they shared, hoping in his absence Ned could contemplate the new situation and get used to the idea. The house's two bedrooms—theirs and their roommate Peggy's—faced the reservoir and the open western sky, as the living room did. They were very yang, with sunlight flooding in the broad windows all afternoon and evening. But the office was on the opposite side, facing the street. It was always cooler and darker than the rest of the house, a yin enclave, a good place to concentrate. Ned's oversize desk and bookshelves and cabinets filled most of the room, and Mason's more utilitarian desk sat in one corner. He sat down, opened his laptop, and set to work.

Resolve your dilemma with Psychic Power!
Personal service. No job too large or small.
Reasonable rates. Los Angeles city, valleys,
Inland Empire.
Pierce the veil of the mystic world to see answers
beyond what your five senses perceive.

That last part is pure genius, he thought. He clicked on "Post."

He had no idea what kind of response he would get, or whether it would get lost in the vast miasma of the Web. He hoped it wouldn't be all cheating spouses and missing cats. The cats would be OK, but he didn't want to be involved in breaking up people's relationships. That sounded more like a job for the firearms type of investigator, following people around and peering in windows.

He started looking at the news online, half reading and half daydreaming. It was understandable that Ned was worried about him leaving his job, but it was also part of the addict personality, getting comfortable and not wanting anything to change. It wasn't really fair to blame Ned for being an addict; he had accepted that up front when they got together. In fact, the twelve-step thing was part of the attraction: if people were really able to live that way, without trying to control each other and just accepting each other as they were, life could be fantastic. But the key was in living it.

Ned had the luxury of working from home and setting his own schedule. In the years they'd been together, Mason had never heard him complain about his work. It certainly wasn't because it was exciting; he worked with bankers and finance companies on something to do with mortgages that Mason could never quite grasp. For Mason, having a full-time job that was essentially gossiping about celebrities meant that the sparkle had worn off fairly quickly. The faces changed every year, but they were always doing the same things, with the same big breasts, the same ripped abs. Mason had grown so tired of being a cog in it that he'd subscribed to *Scientific American* so that he'd have something to read at home that didn't have Hollywood starlets in it. He felt like his life was the opposite of what Ned and other people did: gossip was his work, and science and math were for entertainment.

But not anymore. It was a terrifying thought, not having any income and scrambling for work, but he was on a new path now; he'd have to deal with it as it came up, work or no work, derision or support from Ned. That was a twelve-step thing too, dealing with what was happening now rather than stressing out about the future; he'd try to focus on that.

He unplugged his laptop and carried it into the living room. He wanted to sit on the balcony and enjoy the afternoon sun. It ran the length of the house, connecting the living room and both bedrooms, but the sweet spot was right outside the living room's French doors. The office felt too dark, magnifying his own self-doubt and Ned's dark skepticism. Thinking about it, Mason felt his ire well up again. Why could Ned not just accept it and be supportive?

The idea of the balcony was sweeter than the reality; it was too hot and bright to sit out there at this time of day. He sat on the sofa instead and clicked on his email, and damn, there it was—something from Craigslist. He looked at the time stamp; it had just arrived, twenty-six minutes after the confirmation email for his post. He took this to be a very good sign from the universe and its unseen dimensions: a sign that he was on the right track. Perhaps the world really did need more psychic power.

> Hello,
>
> Can you take cases involving theft? Someone on our staff has been stealing money, and I'm exasperated trying to figure out who it is. Perhaps your psychic power could help. Call me at the number below and we'll see if we can work something out.
>
> Miss Cassie

Excitedly reading it again, he decided that it seemed legit. He couldn't phone her now, of course, as that would tell her he didn't have anything else to do. But this was a great start, and it would help put Ned's mind at ease. And maybe he could let his lingering resentment of Ned's initial reaction melt away.

Ned came in a few minutes later.

"You'll be happy to hear that I already have a lead on a case," Mason said, unable to conceal his excitement. "I have a phone meeting about it this evening." It wasn't really a lie, he reasoned, just an exaggeration, as he did plan to call her later.

"Really?" Ned said, surprised. "That was fast. What kind of case is it?"

"Something about some missing money at a company, I think. I don't have all the details yet. I assume I'll start working on it straight away."

"And how will you be doing that? How will your psychic power manifest itself? With the Ouija board?" He looked dubious.

"Not necessarily," Mason said. "You may not have noticed my psychic abilities, but you've only known me a few years. I took a class when I was at university called Psychic Power, and we studied a whole gamut of techniques to get information that isn't available to the five regular senses."

"Your college had a class called Psychic Power?"

"Well, I was in college at the time, but the class was in an evening adult education program at a public high school. The guy who taught it made his living from doing psychic readings," Mason said.

"And you think you demonstrated psychic power in this class?"

"Oh, yeah. We were doing psychometry—"

"Which is what?"

"You hold an object in your hands, preferably something metal. It has to be something that has been associated with an individual for a while. Keys and jewelry work well. You clear your mind, and information from the object comes in the form of images or sounds that flash into your mind like inspiration. I forget the exact details of the procedure, but I'll look it up on the Web."

Ned looked at him for a moment. "OK, maybe don't tell your clients that you honed your abilities with a Web search."

"It would just be for reference, like a refresher."

"You're not making me feel more confident about this."

"Well, let me finish the story. So we were doing psychometry in the class, and I took this woman's keys to read. I didn't know her or anything about her, except that she knew the validity of psychic power."

Ned bit his lip but nodded for him to continue.

"I closed my eyes, and blanked out my mind, and then I had this sudden image of a bus. On the front of the bus was the number 41. I told her what I'd seen, and she said, 'Oh, my god—I take the number 14 bus every day to get to work.' So I had transposed the digits, but I'd clearly seen her bus."

"OK," Ned said, and thought for a moment. "And that seems like clear evidence of psychic ability to you?"

"Of course it does. If I'd worked at it more, I would have had more details. It's like any craft: you need to practice and sharpen your skills. If I had spent more time with it, I might have seen where she worked, or even what kind of psychological issues she was having."

"Oh, Mason." He sat on the sofa. "So what's the background to these psychic powers, the underlying assumptions? Is it New Age thinking?"

"I'm not sure. What is New Age thinking, exactly?"

Ned was a vociferous nontheist, which for him meant that he had to keep track of theist beliefs. "New Age is the modern Western flavor of religion. It's based on the individual. The state of your life is your own doing, so you can't blame gods and demons. It makes sense that it's the trendy delusion for our society, seeing as we live in a time and place where individuals are empowered. It's an evolutionary step away from the past, when people's lives were completely controlled by a king or a warlord, so religion was based on an angry strongman sitting on a throne somewhere up above."

"OK," Mason said. "For me, this stuff isn't about religion at all. It's actually kind of scientific: the idea is that reality is bigger than we can perceive with our regular senses. I can find some exercises for you to expose your inner senses to it. It's not an exclusive gift, either—anyone can be a psychic. It's like a muscle that you have to work on to develop it."

"That's like saying anyone can be a musician. Lots of people take piano lessons, but not many people are Schubert."

The doorbell rang. "It's Justine," Mason said, hoping Ned would think that was psychic knowledge. He sprang up to open the front door, and there she was, still wearing the summer dress she'd had on at work that morning, her crazy wavy hair pulled back into a loose puff. In her arms she held Mason's banker's box.

"Hey, newly unemployed man," she said. "I brought your stuff."

"Justine," he said, taking the box and setting it on the floor. "I was hoping you'd swing by. Ned, you remember my former colleague?"

"Of course." Ned came to the doorway and embraced her, giving her an air kiss on the cheek.

"I was a little shocked when you left," she said, "but then I heard about your meeting this morning. When you decide to change things up, you don't mess around."

"I didn't really plan it. It just sort of happened," Mason said.

"So are you going to do the psychic thing now?" she said.

Ned looked surprised. "You knew about that?"

"Well, just generally," she said, waving her hand vaguely, not knowing what she'd stepped into. "Mason mentioned it. But I know the frustration of that place. I can feel my soul slowly being destroyed each time I erase a wrinkle on a photo of Cher or Madonna. It's like I can feel the wrinkles actually transferring from their faces to my soul. So maybe I'll use you as an inspiration one of these days, Mason, and fight the power myself."

"I'll let you know how it goes," Mason said. "No regrets so far."

She asked Ned, "How are you feeling about it?"

"Still reeling, but I'll get my balance back soon."

"In the long run, it's good news," she said, and patted him on the shoulder. "He's free now, and he's very brave." She looked at her phone and said, "I need to jet, or the 5 is going to be a parking lot. Call me," she said, waving and walking back out to the street.

By seven o'clock Mason couldn't wait any longer, and he phoned his prospective client. He went into the office so that Ned wouldn't get any more stressed out about his sanity than he already was.

"Hello, ma'am," he said respectfully when she answered. "My name is Mason, and I'm calling about your response to my ad for psychic investigation."

"Oh, thanks for calling back," she said. "I've been tearing my hair out trying to figure this out."

"You said someone is stealing from you?"

"Not from me personally, but from my church. I'm a warden at St. Agatha's Episcopal in Leimert Park, do you know it?"

"Uh, no." He wondered if it would piss Ned off even more if he went to work for a church.

"Well, I'm the people's warden, and one of my duties is to supervise the donations we get and make sure they make it into the bank. I've been trying to figure out why our revenue has fallen, and I think it's disappearing somewhere between the collection plate and the bank deposit."

"Do you have any idea who might be doing it?" he asked.

"That's my problem. Everyone who handles the money is above suspicion, and yet I have clear evidence that donations are going missing. So I've decided I need some outside help. Is this the kind of thing you might be able to work on?"

"I think so," Mason said. "But have you tried to get the police to look into it?"

"I need to have something to show them first," she said. "That's why I contacted you."

"I see. Of course, I'd need more details before I could determine whether I could help you or not."

"I assumed you'd have to come down here and look things over, maybe talk to people," she said.

"Yes, I would. The consultation is free, and we

can discuss my rates after I decide whether I'm able to take the case."

"That sounds reasonable to me. Can we get started on this fairly soon? Before Sunday would be great."

"My schedule is open tomorrow," Mason said. "Would that work?"

They made plans to meet the next day at her church. As he hung up he felt a twinge of anxiety. Would he really be able to perform feats of psychic insight for this woman? But maybe he was just channeling Ned's apprehension, he thought. He hadn't promised her anything, after all, and he didn't really know the details of what was going on yet.

"Did I hear you on the phone?" Ned asked from the kitchen as Mason walked back out. The house dated to the 1950s and was designed in what must have been ultramodern style at the time: the living room and dining room were one broad open space flanked by full-length glass and the balcony. The kitchen was partitioned from this main room only with a countertop, open on both sides, that they called "the bar," even though not much drinking was done there.

"I made an appointment to meet my first client tomorrow," Mason said, sliding onto a barstool.

"That was fast," Ned said. "Stir-fried broccoli and almonds for dinner?" He had already started preparing it.

"Looks great, thanks. Is Peggy going to eat with us?" They often ate with their roommate, but she had a full-time job and an active social life and didn't always make it home until later. One of the things that bonded the three of them was a love of the kitchen and what Ned called "slow eating," meaning dining with conversation and no other distractions, which they did as often as they could. Ned and Mason were both longtime vegans, which had played into their initial attraction. Peggy respected it enough to keep the house vegan. Mason sometimes wondered what she ate when she was out, but whatever it was, over the years she had become an adept vegan cook, like Ned. Mason was less able, but he was supportive of their skills.

"No, she texted," Ned said. "She's not coming back until later, so it's just us."

"Hey, I'm going to need your car tomorrow."

"The Barracuda, I assume? Not possible." He shook his head.

The thing Ned loved most in the world was the Barracuda, a vintage muscle car he kept in pristine condition. Mason knew Ned would say no, but it was worth a shot. "With a new career, one must project the right image to one's clients," Mason said, affecting an academic tone.

"Would one be trying to look like Steve Mc-Queen? That's treading dangerously close to the image of the state-licensed PI with the firearms again. Is your meeting out in the boonies or something?"

"No, it's in Leimert Park."

"That's right in town. You say you hate driving; take your bike."

"That is not the image one wishes to project," Mason said solemnly.

"Well, that's the image you've got." Ned laughed.

"And it's not just that I say I hate driving; I actually do hate driving."

"I know that. There's nothing wrong with not having a car."

"Is that why you have two of them?"

"I like cars," Ned said, sounding annoyed. "And I know that you think people think you're a loser because you don't have a car. But I don't think you're a loser. You are, however, too sensitive."

"Well, that's reassuring."

"It's your issue, toots, not mine." He looked back to the stove and stirred the ingredients in the wok.

Mason held his tongue. In a city built around the automobile it was a reasonable assumption that someone who didn't drive was either physically or financially incapable of it. When people found out that Mason didn't drive, the reaction was usually sympathy or condescension. Sometimes he lied about it, telling people he had narcolepsy and was forbidden by state law from driving, or that his car was in a specialty repair shop in a distant suburb. He'd found that the farther you get from the mainstream, the more work it is to relate to mainstream people. Not driving everywhere was a root assumption in his life, just like eating vegan and sleeping with guys, and it was always slightly jarring when other people didn't get it.

"So what's in Leimert Park?" Ned asked, pulling

Mason's attention back.

He told him about Miss Cassie and the few details of her problems that he knew.

"Has she called the police?" Ned asked.

"I asked her that too, but she said there wasn't anything to show them. It sounds like a fairly nebulous situation. She's suspicious of everybody working there, even though she claims they're all above suspicion."

"She sounds schizophrenic."

"Maybe just overwhelmed," Mason said. "But I can't figure out why a church would want to hire a psychic. It's almost like that would be a conflict of interest."

"You'll have to be careful, stepping over the people rolling around on the floor handling snakes and speaking in tongues."

"It's actually an Episcopal church, which means no snakes. My people were Episcopalians, did I ever tell you that? The wildest thing that happens there is probably some rollicking eighteenth-century hymns. They're very staid and reserved people. I think they even have atheist priests in England."

Ned snorted. "That sounds far-fetched. But did you know there's actually a psychic church? It's one of those nineteenth-century reawakening things in upstate New York. They do the table-rapping and channeling to talk to dead people. They're called Spiritualists."

"I guess I've heard of them. It's kind of a Christian thing, though, right?"

"Yeah, the basic Christian dichotomy: two worlds, the living and the dead, with a god supervising it all."

"You understand that my kind of psychic is different from that, right?" Mason asked.

"I'm glad," Ned said. "I don't think our dining table could handle too much shaking and rapping."

Friday

PEGGY GOT UP BEFORE seven and padded into the kitchen, not bothering to put on her bathrobe because it was already too warm for it. It was almost too warm for her version of pajamas, a tank top and a pair of gray sports shorts. Peggy was fairly tall and wiry. Her day job was working for lawyers, but her passion was music, and she played small gigs almost every weekend under the stage name Peggy Pregnant. When she was performing, her most striking feature, besides her completely fake, extremely pregnant belly, was her long brown hair, which she only let hang straight when she was on stage. It gave her a 1960s look, which worked remarkably well with her folky music and acoustic guitar. This early in the morning she had her hair tied casually behind her neck, but by the time she got to her nine-to-five grind it was usually piled elaborately on top of her head and held in place with a hairpin.

"Where's Mason?" she asked, and sat at the bar across from Ned. "He's going to be late for work."

"Three guesses," he said.

"Sleeping. Is it Saturday? There's no way I could have slept through a whole Friday. My office would have called."

"He blew up at his boss and quit his job yesterday. Bam, no more income for Mason."

"Wow," she said, rubbing her eyes, and then added, "But that's actually great news."

"You think?" Ned said, and passed her a cup of coffee.

"He hated that job. He's been talking about moving on pretty much since he started there."

"OK, true, but he's not going to go get another job. He's decided to become a professional psychic." He stood with both hands firmly braced on the bar and waited for her reaction.

"Seriously? Is he going to open a storefront, like those neon crystal-ball places on the Westside?"

"I don't think so. You'll have to ask him about the details. He's already set up some meeting with a potential client. It sounds more like he wants to be a private detective."

"It sounds like you're worried," she said.

"I'm trying to deal with it without freaking out. One day at a time, like they say in program," he said.

MASON SLEPT AS LATE as possible when he didn't have to get up; he wasn't a morning person and saw no reason to fight it. Accordingly, he had set his meeting with Miss Cassie for the early afternoon. Ned was already in the office working when he rolled out of bed and made his first pot of espresso. It took him at least an hour to become functional, regardless of when he woke up. Ned had once suggested that Mason was on Honolulu time; when given the choice, he got up around the time most people there did, three hours after LA.

"Coffee?" he shouted down the hall.

"No, thanks," Ned called back. "When's your meeting?"

"I'm leaving soon."

He ate some fruit and wondered whether he should wear something dressy, maybe even a necktie. He was going to a church, after all. But finally he decided to wear what he was comfortable in—a collared short-sleeved shirt, along with cargo shorts—and hopefully that energy would help his potential client relax too. Even in the darkest part of winter he rarely wore long pants, except when an extremely cold evening forced the issue. Southern California had such good weather, he reasoned, it made no sense to hide from it.

The midday sun blazed gloriously, as usual, when he stepped outside. It was a short ride from their hillside pad down to the metro station in their neighborhood. He had decided not to take his bicycle all the way, and locked it up at the station; St. Agatha's Episcopal was only twenty minutes' walk from the metro.

The metro is the city's great leveler. Unlike the bus, used almost exclusively by the poorest five percent of the population, the train usually had a reasonable cross-section of classes and ethnicities. It made sense, Mason thought; there was more room, and less stopping and starting, which made it more comfortable. Despite his feeling inadequate from time to time about being carless in a car-oriented city, it really was mostly by choice. He had had a car for a while, but as the rail network expanded and his desire to be out running around chasing guys and being social leveled off, he finally got rid of it. At first it felt daring and bohemian, and he explained it to friends as something he'd chosen to do because he really was part of the disenfranchised underclass.

"Underclass people don't summer in France," Peggy had said. Although he'd only done that a couple of times when the dollar was high against the euro, he knew she was right, and he had to revise the story.

Leimert Park is one of those urban neighborhoods that reflect the dramatic changes in twentieth-century American society. Platted in the 1920s and 1930s as a model community for working-class whites, it became primarily African American after the courts ended real estate segregation in the late

1940s. It was still eighty percent black today, but Latinos were gradually becoming a bigger part of the population. Mason didn't get down there very often, and when he got off the metro and started walking south, he remembered how different it was from his the neighborhoods where he spent his time—Hollywood, Silver Lake, and Downtown. Fast-food joints crowded every commercial block here, to the total exclusion of other food options. The problem was so severe that the city council had slapped a moratorium on new fast-food outlets for all of South LA. But veering onto the residential side streets revealed delightful 1930s apartment buildings, tidy Spanish bungalows with well-tended lawns and flowerbeds, and broad grassy medians that people in more central neighborhoods could only dream about.

Soon St. Agatha's appeared ahead, a 1960s-era modernist structure with a sharply peaked roof and a small unadorned spire. When he got near he saw that it looked closed up, understandable for a smallish church on a Friday afternoon, but the side door was indeed unlocked when he pulled on it, as Miss Cassie had said it would be.

He opened the door without stepping in. Someone once told him that tall guys come in two configurations: string bean and rugby. Mason stood 6 foot 2 and definitely had the rugby body, so he'd had a lifetime to learn how intimidating he could be without even trying. He made a habit of giving other people lots of space until they were better acquainted.

"Hello?" he ventured.

A woman came toward the door. "You must be Mason," she said. "Come on in." He stepped up into the room, clearly the church's kitchen. "I'm Miss Cassie," she said with a broad smile, looking him directly in the eye and shaking his hand.

She's had marketing training, he thought, and tried to make more mental notes about her, not knowing what might be important later. She was a little older, maybe in her early fifties, fairly tall, and slightly full-figured, although her dark tailored suit with its knee-length skirt did a good job of deemphasizing that. Custom tailoring: that probably meant money. Her eyeglasses looked expensive too.

"A pleasure to meet you, ma'am." Mason wasn't really a formal person, but her somewhat formal presence told him to use polite language. And anyone who introduces herself with a title like "Miss" probably expects some degree of formality.

"We can talk in the office, but let me show you the nave and the altar." He followed her through a doorway and across the back of the church. "This is our sanctuary," she said, pride in her voice. The austere altar at the front was draped in green, the color for the long season between Pentecost and Advent, Mason remembered. Even the pulpit was prim, nothing more than a lectern made of the same light wood as the pews, the altar rail, and the wall paneling. Behind the pulpit was a similarly plain desk with a modern keyboard and a stool; the church organ, he realized, but it was only a keyboard with some cables running to the wall, not connected to any speakers that he could see. The only real color in the room was the red carpeting, as the high windows were undecorated clear glass.

"Low church, if I'm not mistaken?" Mason said. Low Anglicans did things more simply, like the Scandinavian Protestants, while high Anglicans retained the ornate trappings of the Roman Catholics.

"Very good," she said, her eyebrows rising. "Most American Anglicans are high church, but we're a newer congregation. It can be a mixture from year to year, depending on who the vicar is."

"My people were high church, but that just meant there was padding on the kneelers."

She laughed appreciatively, and he knew he had made at least a small connection.

"Were you confirmed into the church?"

"Yes, but I must say I haven't been involved for many years."

Miss Cassie nodded, then gestured and started to walk up the central aisle. They had been standing near a tall narrow table with a dish of water in the top. It reminded him of the water provided for visitors to purify themselves at temples and shrines in Asia. His hands were a bit sticky, he realized, from riding the train and walking in the heat, and before following her he dipped them into the water, rubbed them together, and wiped them on his shirt, discretely under his arms. It was so warm and dry, the water would completely evaporate before anyone even noticed the hand prints, he reasoned. Miss Cassie had half turned around to see what he was doing.

"I guess it has been a while since you were in a church," she said.

Mason's cheeks reddened. He looked back at the water stand. "Oh … is that a holy-water dish?"

"We don't call it a dish; it's called the stoup. And yes, it's blessed water." She pronounced the phrase *blessed water* carefully, as if talking to a nonnative speaker of English, or an eight-year-old. "People use it to cross themselves when they come in."

"Sorry about that," he said. "I remember some of the rituals, but not everything. Coming back into a church must have clogged up my aura."

"That would explain a lot," she said. "Let's hope there's no permanent damage done to your aura here today." She turned and led him along the central aisle toward the altar. At the side of the room a doorway opened to a set of two small offices, and beyond them was a dark cavernous room; the church hall, he assumed. In the first office, beside cluttered storage shelves, bookcases, and file cabinets, was a big desk covered with piles of paper and books. Miss Cassie sat behind the desk and motioned for Mason to sit in one of the chairs in front. A bulky handbag sprawled open on one side of the desk; it must be hers, he thought. He slid off his backpack as he sat down and pulled out a yellow notepad and a pen.

"It's certainly more yin back here," Mason said, looking around.

She didn't respond to that, but asked, "Do you have a business card?"

"No, not on me," Mason said, patting his shirt

pocket as if he'd forgotten to bring them. "But I can give you my contact information, and references, if you need them."

"I don't suppose that'll be necessary. But can I ask your surname?"

"Braithwaite," Mason said.

"That does sound high church."

"Not in England, actually. I've been told it's an immigrant name there because it came with the Danes nine hundred years ago."

She smiled and nodded, looking him over. Mason realized she was in the process of assessing him, which made him slightly nervous.

"So, Miss Cassie, can I ask you why a church would hire a psychic?"

"Because praying didn't help," she said, her face deadpan. He wasn't sure whether to laugh or to nod understandingly, but she cracked a smile and said, "I'm kidding. Listen, I'm a humanist, and a scientist, and I know that's where the answer to any problem will be found. But I grew up around here, and I have friends here that I've known all my life. St. Agatha's is my community. So even though I'm not really religious, I'm part of this place, and I help take care of it."

"I understand." On his notepad he wrote discreetly "humanist" and "scientist."

"My personal thinking is that science hasn't figured out everything that exists in nature yet," she said. "In the nineteenth century, most scientists didn't believe powered flight was possible, and today you can fly anywhere in the world. So whatever you call it, your psychic ability or your sixth sense, it probably has an explanation that will fit into the scientific framework."

"That's great, Miss Cassie," he said, and nodded emphatically. "My thinking runs along the same lines."

"The world is far too complex to have firm opinions about what's possible and impossible," she said.

"It's refreshing to hear that. Most people seem to have their minds made up already." He shifted position in the chair, and then said, "So you're having trouble with theft."

"Yes." She looked around at the piles of paper on the desk and shook her head.

"On the phone you said you were the people's warden. In medieval times part of that job was guarding the church's silver."

"It still is, Mason. Legally, I'm the guardian of all of the parish's property. I'm one of only three people who have the combination to that safe over there, along with the vicar and the rector's warden. We don't have much in the way of plate, like churches did back then, but I am responsible for the modern equivalent, the money."

He scribbled on his pad and said, "You also said you had proof that money was going missing?"

"See these?" She handed him a sheaf of small pale-yellow envelopes, maybe three by five inches in size. Printed on the flap of the first one was "September – 3rd Sunday," and below that on the body of the envelope, "Miss Cassandra Millar."

"They're tithing envelopes," she said, "and we have them personalized for regular congregation members. They place them in the collection plate on Sunday with their donation tucked inside. We don't really keep track of who's paying what, but I know most of the regular congregants well enough to remember that they were here on a given Sunday, and of course they always put an envelope in the collection plate. I've tried to keep this whole business quiet—who wants to hear that one of their church administrators is a thief?—but I asked a couple of people whose envelopes were missing when we counted the offerings, and they swore up and down that they had put their envelope in as usual."

"OK," Mason said, still taking notes, "so at what point did you first notice the tithing envelopes had gone missing?"

She sighed. "That's why I wanted somebody from the outside. I can't be suspicious of any of these people. They're all good decent folks. I don't know how long it's been going on, but at least six months."

"Who passes the collection plates?"

"It used to be teenagers in the congregation. I'd recruit whoever was there that Sunday and dressed nicely. But I got suspicious, so I made it into a job for the adults. Now the same two guys do it every week, Michael and Justin. I told them that they had to fill out an employee card because they were handling money, even though they don't get paid. I thought that if either one of them was involved in skulduggery, recording all their personal details might scare them off." She stood and walked over to one of the file cabinets, opened it with a key, and pulled out a thick folder. "Here they are," she said, sitting down again and passing him two sheets from the file. Stapled to each was a head-shot photo of a smiling young man wearing a white shirt and tie, posed somewhere in the church and looking into the camera, obviously taken at close range, perhaps with a phone. On each sheet was a list of personal details: home address, driver's license number, family members.

"Did you run any checks on these two?" he asked.

"Only a cursory criminal records check, and a credit check; that's really all I could get away with as an employer."

He copied down their names and a few other details. "And after they pass the plates, where does the money go then?"

"They place the plates on the altar, one on top of the other, and the vicar covers them with a cloth during the Eucharist. The plates sit there until the end of the service, which is just a minute or two later."

"Do you have an employee file on this vicar?"

"Oh, god, no. That's all handled by the diocese. Reverend Kaleni has been with us for several years now, and he's above any suspicion."

"But therein lies your problem, Miss Cassie, and that's why you've called me in. Good people can do bad things when presented with the right opportunity," he said, knitting his brow in an attempt to appear earnest and experienced.

"I really don't think he could be involved. He cares about this community and works hard for us. He's originally South African, but he's not socially conservative like some of the African Anglicans are. The parish loves him. He's a little old guy, about this tall," she said, holding her hand out at shoulder level.

Mason didn't quite understand how stature or age could correlate with guilt and innocence, but he could tell that she didn't want to distrust the vicar, which revealed her own limitations on the matter: she couldn't be objective about it.

"Have you checked him out?" he asked.

She looked at him for a moment before answering. "Yes, I ran a couple of records checks. There wasn't anything untoward."

"OK. What happens to the money after the vicar covers it up?" Mason asked.

"When the service ends, the vicar steps out of the chancel, and the rector's warden steps in and takes the plates, still covered with a cloth, and carries them back here into the offices. The rector's warden is Mrs. Lewis—Betty Lewis—and again, there's no way she could be involved. I've known her forever. She and I do the church's books together, and she helped me figure out that someone was stealing from us in the first place."

"Have you looked into her at all?"

Miss Cassie hesitated, as if reluctant to go into an unpleasant topic, and said, "She's my friend."

"That doesn't mean she's incapable of committing a crime," he said. "I don't want to be rude, but I think that's why you brought me here. And something tells me you did look into her."

"Yes, I did." She sighed. "Her husband has been involved in some questionable real estate dealings in Orange County"—she pronounced the last two words as if they were inherently distasteful—"but Betty was never implicated, at least not according to the newspaper. Their personal credit is clean, and they have money. She wouldn't need to pilfer the comparatively petty sums that show up in our collection plates."

"Need isn't the only reason people steal," Mason said, meeting her eye in what he hoped was a meaningful way as he wrote on his pad.

"True, but again, I just can't believe she's capable of something like that."

"Is she left alone with the collection plates?"

"I meet her in here right after she picks them up. Sometimes I get in here before she does. We take the cloth off and start counting the donations, always the two of us. We open the envelopes and fill out a deposit slip that lists the checks. We write the totals in the ledger. We've only recently been counting and filling out a deposit slip right away on Sunday; before that I think cash was probably disappearing between Sunday and the day we made the deposit. I've also started using locking deposit bags, like retailers do. So now everything goes into the bag, and it gets locked. The bag sits in the safe, also locked, until Monday or Tuesday, when Betty or I get around to depositing it at the bank."

Mason quickly added to his notes:

Who handles the money?
- Michael and Justin (pass the plates), clean records
- vicar (handles the plates), record?
- Betty Lewis (counts the take), no record
- deposit slip on Sun.
- locked deposit bag in safe
- bank it Mon. or Tues.

"Does the deposit tally with the initial count in the ledger?"

"It does now, since I've been locking everything up. But even though cash isn't going missing after we count it anymore, the tithing envelopes have gone missing by the time we're sitting here opening them. It just doesn't make any sense."

"Who has keys to the deposit bag?"

"Only Betty and me."

He spent a few moments completing his notes, and then said, "So it boils down to the two guys who pass the collection plates, the vicar, you, and Mrs. Lewis."

"Except for me. I'm the one who called you here. Why would I do that if I was the thief?"

"Let's not rule anything out until we do some research," Mason said gravely.

She looked at him for a moment, then laughed and shook her head. "Fine. Maybe it's me."

"Have you inspected the altar and the paten and all that to make sure these envelopes aren't getting misplaced there?"

"Of course we did, and there's no way that could happen. It's just a table with a little cloth draped over it."

"Do you mind if I have a look?"

"That's why you're here." She stood up, and they walked back into the church. It was brightly lit by the afternoon sun streaming in the high windows. She lifted the gate in the altar rail. She was right: there was nowhere to misplace or hide anything on the altar. Mason whisked off the altar cloth and examined it; it was simple, thin fabric with no hidden pockets or folds. He got on all fours to look under the altar. Again, it was just a simple piece of wood on a pedestal, with nowhere to hide anything. He considered doing a hands-on reading of the altar, but he didn't think it would have worked, as it was made of wood, and metals are the best conductors of psychic energy. Plus, despite declaring herself a secularist, he suspected that Miss Cassie would consider a psychic reading of the altar to be somewhat sacrilegious.

"I think I know how to approach this case," he said, standing up and replacing the altar cloth. "There are several things I can do to get psychic insight into who's stealing from you, and I'm pretty sure I can get a clear answer." It was partly bluster but partly true. There were several things he could try, but he had no idea whether he could figure it out.

"Good," she said. "But before we start on that, what is it going to cost me?"

"Five hundred a day up front, plus expenses,"

he said, trying to sound resolute. He had seen that number once at work in an article about a private detective who stalked unfaithful celebrities.

"OK, there's no way that's going to happen." She shook her head. "Way, way out of range. We're a little church in South LA, not the Crystal Cathedral."

He nodded. "How about two hundred bucks if I figure it out, nothing if I don't, no expenses unless I clear them with you first?"

"You know, I think I can work with that," she said, and he wondered whether she was trying to suppress a smile. "And I'll pay you a bonus if somebody gets arrested."

"Cool," he said, and stuck out his right hand. She shook it and couldn't hold back a laugh. Mason wasn't sure what was funny.

"So what's your plan of attack?" she asked.

"I'll need to examine the safe. It doesn't have to be open; I just need to read its energy. I'd like to see the deposit bag as well. And after that, we can look into your employee files a little more thoroughly."

They walked back into the office, and Miss Cassie crouched daintily in front of the safe. She twirled the dial, carefully blocking his view of it with her body. He had glanced at it earlier, but up close it was suspiciously elaborate, considering her claim that the parish had only humble resources. Why would they need such a big safe? It also looked old, certainly predating the building it was in by decades, with an antiquated brass handle and dial. It was painted solid black, and the gold pinstripes and old-timey lettering that spelled out "Montclair Security" were cracked and faded.

She pulled the heavy door open and took out a small green canvas bag with a heavy zipper and lock. Inside the safe he could see stacks of paperwork and some silver and gold objects, probably plated chalices, patens, and candlesticks of only moderate value. "Here's the deposit bag," she said. "Now, what do you need to do?"

"I'm going to sit here with it for a minute," he said. "You can stay, of course, but I'll need silence."

"I'll be right over here," she said, and sat behind the desk. She took a tablet out of her purse, flipped it open, and started tapping on it.

Mason sat in front of the desk again but turned the chair so that he wasn't facing her. He put the deposit bag in his lap, but he didn't pick it up yet. He needed to prepare the conduit to what he'd called the "mystic world" in his ad, but was much more accurately described as "greater reality." His thinking was that the physical world we experience every day is just a tiny part of a vast and limitless reality that we choose to focus on. All around us swirl, unseen, the potential matter, energy, and probabilities that sometimes coalesce into our physical reality. Everything that exists in our world was once waiting in that grand cloud, and remains connected to it; the goal for a psychic is to tap into that information, to gain insight into how things in the physical world are interconnected. Right now, his plan was to pick up the energy of the green deposit bag and find out if anyone had been messing with it.

He closed his eyes and tried to clear his mind. It's harder than it sounds; anyone who has tried meditation knows how random thoughts pop into consciousness unbidden, especially when you try to ignore or suppress them. It took a few minutes, but eventually his mind was dark, calm, and quiet. His eyes still closed, he picked up the bag and held the metal lock between his palms. Practically speaking, the trick with psychometry is to distinguish true information connected to the object from random background thoughts.

Slowly, into the blank expanse of his mind, came the image of a dark, throbbing mass. It became clearer and pulsated regularly, like a heart-beat. He realized that it was a heart, and he almost lost the image because he was so excited to be see-ing it. But he managed to hold on to the image, and it stabilized. The spiderweb of veins around the heart became darker, and the organ throbbed more quickly. He felt a definite sense of panic—not in himself, but from the image. Gradually it faded away.

He opened his eyes and turned to Miss Cassie. "Has anyone in the parish died recently?"

She looked up from her tablet. "Not in the last year or so, no," she said. "But you look like you've just been boiled."

Mason touched his cheek. "Redheads tend to turn red easily," he said. "How about someone with heart trouble, or a heart attack?"

She knotted her eyebrows and thought for a moment. "Not that I've heard of. People often discuss their health issues with the vicar, and he asks us to pray for them here during Sunday service. But I haven't heard of anyone with that kind of problem lately."

Although it had been a clear image, it wasn't a great lead. He'd always known how difficult it was to interpret the information gleaned from supernatural sources. Maybe Ned's comparison with Schubert was accurate; this case required well-developed skills, but he still felt like a beginner. In a flash of dark self-doubt he thought about how limited his experience really was: some general impressions and obtuse images gleaned from people and objects at a few parties. But it always felt important, and real. Interpreting the images was going to be the real challenge.

He sighed. "OK, I'm going to read the safe now. As before, I must request complete silence."

Miss Cassie chuckled and nodded, looking back to her tablet. He pushed the safe's heavy door closed and knelt in front of it. Once again he worked to clear his mind and focus on an empty point in the center of his head. When his mind was quiet, he put his hands on either side of the box.

It took a few minutes, but an image formed. He saw a row of desks in an office; beside the desks were tall windows with venetian blinds. An oversize bouquet of flowers sat on a room-length credenza, and men in formal suits sat at most of the desks. There were a few women as well, also dressed formally. Mason had the impression that it was a long time ago, perhaps when the safe was new.

"Well," he said, standing up and turning to Miss Cassie, "I think the next step is to have a look at the employee files again."

"No inspiration from the great beyond?"

"I got lots of information, but it doesn't all fit together yet. Things have to percolate." He waggled his fingers vaguely beside his head.

"I guess it would have been too easy just to get a name," she said, opening the fat file again and handing him the two pages on the collection stewards.

"Actually, would you mind terribly if I went through the whole file on my own? I won't mess anything up, and I'll keep it all in order. I might get some incidental insight that way."

"I guess that would be OK, as long as you treat everything as confidential. Privacy laws, and all that. The top drawer of the file cabinet is all about employees and parishioners."

"Confidential, of course. I know all about that." He nodded for emphasis. As she stood up and flipped her tablet cover closed, once again she suppressed a smile.

"And if anybody asks," she said, "you're a paid consultant hired to help me with some staffing problems. Nobody needs to know any more about it than that."

"Discretion it is," he said.

She gathered up her handbag and said, "I'm going to sit in the next office and make some phone calls. Shout if you need me."

"Of course." Paid consultant, he thought. He liked the sound of that.

At first he concentrated on the photos and data sheets on Michael and Justin. He couldn't use psychometry on a sheet of paper, but he tried to open his energy channels to whatever inspiration might be available. He didn't really get any impressions about them, but he noticed that Michael certainly had childish handwriting, considering he claimed to have a master's degree.

He dug into the first file, which seemed to be mostly the research Miss Cassie had done in the last few months. There were credit reports on the two young men as well as on the vicar, on Mrs. Lewis, and a couple of other people. Michael had had a lot of dealings with banks and financial institutions in San Diego rather than locally, but that wasn't all that strange; perhaps he had grown up there.

He pulled other files out of the top drawer and dug through them. Nothing stood out as significant, and after half an hour he was not getting any psychic vibes about any of it. One folder had a bunch of photos in it from an event, obviously held next door in the church hall, possibly a wedding reception or a party. He flipped through the photos, looking at the faces, and stopped at one that seemed familiar. It was a young woman, in her twenties, and like the other parishioners, she wore formal attire. Her jaw line and her eyes were unmistakable. He flipped the photo over, and sure enough, someone had written "Sherri Millar / Davis wedding."

"Miss Cassie, is this your daughter?" he shouted to her through the doorway to the adjoining office.

"What?" She came in and looked down at the photo. "I don't know what that's doing in there." She took it from his hand and folded it in half.

"Ooh, it's really hard to get creases out of photo paper," he said, but she seemed not to hear. "Is she still part of the congregation?"

"No, she's not. And you needn't be concerned about her."

"But she is your daughter?"

"She was. She left here and cut me out of her life ages ago. But that's not your business, and she has nothing to do with the matter at hand." There was an edge in her voice, which Mason took as a clear warning to let it go.

"I understand," he said. "Listen, I'm not picking up much extrasensory information from these files. I think the next step is for me to come here on Sunday and observe the service, and perhaps meet some of the players."

"I thought you might want to do that. Do you have a suit?"

"I'm not sure if it still fits, but I could scare one up."

"Well, wear it. Your options are to sit in the congregation, out in the open, as if you were a guest. Not my guest, of course, as that would invite too many questions, but just someone who wanted to go to church. You'd be undercover, in a way, but out in the open. And there would be three hundred pairs of eyes on you the whole time."

"Because I'm an outsider?"

"Partly that, but mostly because the congregation is almost completely African American, and you're as pink as Barbie's convertible. The neighborhood isn't as uniform as it once was, but that's who we are," she said, and added gently, "As a visitor, you'd be more than welcome, but you'd stand out."

"And what's the other option?" he asked.

"You could hide in the organ loft and watch everything from up there."

"That sounds less stressful. Can we look at it?"

They went through the office's other door into the church hall, which was as big as the church itself. Near the back was a narrow set of stairs leading up; at the top was a high loft, above the back of the church, that housed the pipe organ. That explained why there were no speakers mounted in the church, and just a simple keyboard for the organist. The tallest pipes of the organ itself were perhaps ten feet tall and stretched nearly to the ceiling. Below the pipes, the unit's boxy base was at least six feet long and three feet high. It was faced with ornately carved wood that looked old, perhaps dating from the 1920s. At the top of the stairs, between the organ and where the sharply sloping ceiling met the wall, were a few feet of floor space. There was a protective railing and a bird's-eye view of the altar and most of the pews. Only the foyer was out of sight directly below the loft. He hadn't even noticed it from below, so he knew it would make a great place to go unseen.

"The keyboard for the organ is up front, so no one ever comes up here," Miss Cassie explained. "It stays dark, so you wouldn't be noticed, and I'll make sure the door at the bottom of the stairs is shut. The organ might get a bit loud, though, and it might be warm so close to the ceiling."

"I wonder why such a Spartan church was built with an elaborate pipe organ?" he asked. "And why did they hide it up here?"

"It wasn't planned that way. It was moved from an older church that was deconsecrated in the 1950s. The organ didn't have a place to go, and they wanted to keep it in the diocese, so it was installed here as an afterthought, probably because St. Agatha's didn't have its own organ then. The designer of this building was definitely low church, but it was moved in here after he was finished with the project. It's strange, I think, to have such a carefully decorated thing hidden away up here. I'm surprised no one ever wanted to reclaim it and move it somewhere more prominent."

"Maybe the diocese forgot about it."

"Perhaps. I'm glad if they did, though, because it sounds lovely."

He looked around the loft and nodded. "This is probably the best solution," he said. "And at the end of the service I could go down into the office to watch the counting procedure."

"Let's plan on that, then. You'll have to walk through the hall to get back to the offices, but nobody should be in there yet. In the office it'll just be me and Mrs. Lewis, so you won't have to worry about staying out of sight." He followed her back down the stairs to the hall, and she closed the door behind them.

"What time does the service start?" he asked.

"At ten, which means people are here setting up at nine, which means I'll let you in at eight. I'll leave the kitchen door open, just like today."

Ouch, he thought, that meant a very early start. But there was no other way.

MASON LEFT ST. AGATHA'S and walked back to the main square that anchored the neighborhood, a patch of grass with some shade trees and benches fronted by shops. He found a coffee place, where he slammed a double espresso before walking back toward the metro. He needed the caffeine; psychometry took a lot of energy.

He realized he was satisfied with the meeting with Miss Cassie. She trusted him, he could tell, which put added pressure on him to come up with an answer for her. At least he hadn't promised anything. He was worried about performing, of course, because this was his first gig. But he had the feeling that this psychic power business was going to work out. Whether he solved the case or not, it felt like he was doing something right.

PEGGY WAS OUT FOR the evening, so Ned and Mason made dinner together. This usually meant Ned did the work, and Mason sat at the bar and chatted. Ned enjoyed cooking so he let it slide, happy to have the company.

"What can I do?" Mason asked as he walked into the kitchen. Ned was working on the dough for a pizza.

"You can pull up a stool and tell me all about your meeting today."

"Sure, but I can help cook first."

Ned looked up, surprised. Mason was usually too wiped out after work to even pretend to be interested in helping to cook. "There are three peppers in the bottom of the fridge. You could slice them up. But wash them first."

Mason pulled out the peppers, red and yellow, and ran them under the tap. "Such pretty colors," he said, and put them on the cutting board. "Which knife?"

"You want one with heft, because it's not detailed work. So use the biggest one."

Mason pulled open the knife drawer and selected the longest chef's knife. He began tentatively cutting a pepper. Ned dusted a pizza stone with flour and started pounding out the dough.

"You can leave the tip of the knife on the board, and just lift the handle. You can build up some speed too if you kind of make it bounce."

"Cool," Mason said, changing technique and chopping with more confidence.

"It's like a new you, getting in on making dinner."

"I guess I'm not feeling brain-dead today. Usually it takes me the whole weekend to recover from work. I feel kind of energized."

Ned assembled the peppers and some tomatoes on the pizza and put it in to bake. After he pulled it out of the oven, they ate at the dining table, next to the bar. Mason talked about meeting

Miss Cassie and St. Agatha's.

"I can't believe you're actually doing this," Ned said, "and that someone is taking you seriously."

Mason bristled. "Just because you don't believe that I'm psychic doesn't mean no one else does."

"No need for hostility," Ned said, holding up both hands. "I was just making an observation."

"Well," he said, trying to get calm again, "she's definitely taking me seriously. I really think that getting this job is positive reinforcement, like the universe telling me that I'm on the right track. That has to be a good sign."

"You never really said how you found this client," Ned said.

"On a professional website," Mason said. "Kind of a job-sharing thing." It wasn't really a lie, he thought, although he knew it was a bit of an obfuscation. He had to consider Ned's anxiety level, and not mentioning the free-for-all scam-ridden classified ads was really more of a kindness to him. He also knew that presenting Ned with the plain truth without the spin might make him look foolish, and who needed that? He felt judged often enough as it was.

"Do you think you'll do some other kind of marketing?"

"Eventually, sure. First I just need to get some business cards, though. I wished I'd had one today."

"What are you going to list as your job title?"

"Psychic investigator, I think. It's how you're going to have to introduce me from now on: 'This is my boyfriend, the psychic investigator.'"

"I think I can do that," he said, and smiled. "But let me get used to the idea first."

ANOTHER INVALUABLE WEAPON IN the psychic arsenal that Mason had learned back in college was lucid dreaming, and he was hopeful that it would give him insight into the troubles at St. Agatha's. The key with lucid dreaming is to become aware, during a dream, that you're dreaming, and then to actively manipulate the experience. Some people who became skilled at it were able, during a lucid dream, to astrally project their minds out of their bodies and visit other parts of the world, other times, or their other incarnations. He wasn't sure that he could pull off a feat like that, especially since he hadn't practiced for ages, but before falling asleep that night he gave himself the suggestion that he would have an insightful lucid dream. He also put a pad and pen in the nightstand drawer so that he could write down anything important when he woke up, before it slipped away.

"Wake up inside the dream," he said under his breath as he lay in bed, near the point of drifting into sleep.

"What?" Ned said, rolling over beside him.

"Nothing," he said. "Sleepy time."

He wasn't really able to become self-aware during his dreams that night, but one of them was more vivid than usual, and he remembered it clearly. It was also slightly disturbing, like dreams he remembered having when the dentist gave him pain meds after working on his wisdom teeth. He was in a sparkly nightclub, with bright white spot-lights reflecting on shiny surfaces everywhere. He was on a stage and playing an electric guitar. In reality he couldn't play any instrument, but in the dream he sounded great. The problem was that the strings of the guitar were really tight, and every time he plucked one it hurt his fingers. But he kept at it, because he was on stage and people were watching.

He wrote down the key points and images on his notepad when he woke up, but really, he thought, it didn't seem to be anything to do with St. Agatha's.

Saturday

OR SATURDAY THEY'D PLANNED a kitchen day, a regular event for the three of them. Ned wanted to can tomatoes, Peggy wanted to make almond milk, and Mason wanted someone to make a cake. Ned was up and in the kitchen making breakfast early, before the day started getting hot. Peggy wandered in, sleep in her eyes.

"Muesli and fruit?" Ned offered.

"Oh, yeah, that sounds great. Have you made coffee?"

"Oh, you know I have. No need to be polite," he said, and poured her a cup.

"So how's your 'keep calm and carry on' thing

going, with Mason's new career?" she asked.

"It's actually OK," he said. "He found a client already on a website, and she hired him."

"Is it to talk to her dead relatives or something?"

"No, this woman works for some church in South LA. He's going to try to find out who's stealing from their office, something like that."

"Not that big one in West Adams? They've been mired in scandal lately, if you believe the newspaper."

"No, it's a little one in Leimert Park."

"I like that neighborhood," she said. "There's a big blues club there. I've never played it, but when I dated that sax player we used to go down there all the time."

"I remember that guy."

"But Mason's actually going to find a thief using psychic power? That sounds more like Sam Spade than a Ouija-board jockey."

"I know, right? He assures me it's completely safe, but I wonder. At least something's happening, though, and it's not just a pipe dream."

WHEN HE GOT OUT of bed, Mason could smell the tomatoes cooking. He found Ned in the kitchen, wearing an apron that was already stained with blotches of red.

"It looks like tomato carnage," he said, kissing Ned on the cheek before firing up the espresso machine.

"I wanted to get the skins off, and it got a little messy."

"Where's Peggy?"

"She's here," Ned said. "We had breakfast together. I think she's in her room."

Mason walked down to her bedroom. "Hey, Peggy," he said, poking his head in through her open door. She sat cross-legged on the floor in front of a cardboard moving box, its contents stacked around her.

"What's all this?" he asked.

"More of my mom's stuff," she said. Her mother had died less than a year ago, not even sixty, a victim of breast cancer. It had been a devastating loss, and Peggy, an only child, had relied on her roommates a lot for emotional support. It had made them all closer.

"How are you doing with it?"

"I have to go into it a little at a time, and not before I'm ready. It seems to become possible in stages. A month ago I couldn't have looked at this."

"Anything interesting?"

"Interesting and frustrating. Look at this." She handed him a yellowing, official-looking document. It was a birth certificate, he realized, and then he saw that it was hers.

"You were born in Lakewood? What's in Lakewood?"

"Dude, that's not the point. Focus! Look at the box for 'Father of Child.'"

It was marked "Unknown."

"Did your mother really not know, or was it that she just didn't want to say?"

"I know she knew," Peggy said, "and she got

agitated whenever I pressed her about it or even mentioned it. I probably started asking as soon as I could talk, but it never got me anywhere. Eventually I just let it go. Maybe I thought she'd tell me one day, when she was ready, or on her deathbed or something. But I was with her when she was on her deathbed, and she never told me, and now ... it's too late." Her face crinkled into a sad smile.

"It's too late to hear it from her, but that doesn't mean you can't find out some other way."

"That's what I'm hoping. Maybe there'll be something in all these papers."

"Let's go make almond milk," he said, "and tell Ned about it."

Their espresso machine made one eight-ounce pot at a time, enough for three or four dainty little individual shots, but Mason always poured the whole pot into a big mug and considered it a cup of coffee. Because it was so warm in the kitchen, he took a couple of ice cubes from the dispenser in the fridge door and dropped them in the cup, then plunked down on one of the stools at the bar. Peggy slipped into the kitchen beside Ned and put on an apron.

"Why, Peggy, as I live and breathe," Ned said with exaggerated delight.

"Edgar," she replied in the same tone. Mason wasn't sure why, but she often called Ned by his full name. To him the name Edgar sounded stodgy and Anglo, but it was actually popular in Latin America. In effect, the abbreviation Ned was a reanglicization, an embodiment of language pragmatism in California.

"Did you know that Peggy's mom had so many gentleman callers that she couldn't figure out which one was her father?" Mason said.

"Really?" Ned said, looking at her quizzically. "I guess I knew you didn't really have a dad."

"I never had one growing up, but obviously there has to be a biological father. And she wasn't oblivious as to who it was," Peggy said. She poured the soaking water off her bowl of almonds and started putting them into the blender. "I think it was something that was painful for her. Maybe the guy broke her heart. She was young when she had me."

"She never said anything about who he was?" Ned said. He had started ladling his tomatoes into canning jars.

"Her birth certificate doesn't say," Mason said.

"No. She would never even talk about it. I know she worked in bars and had some wild years back in the seventies and eighties, but I don't think she was ever a drunk or a junkie. I could see how a junkie might not remember who she'd slept with, but I knew my mother, and she wasn't clueless like that. She knew, but she just didn't want to deal with it." She put the blender container under the tap and filled it partway with water. "But as a result, she was the only family I ever knew. I feel like an orphan."

"It makes sense that you'd want to find out about him," Ned said.

"Yeah. I think it's become important to me now because she's gone. Knowing who he was would give me something else, more history."

"I know how that feels," Ned said. "Not knowing is worse than any information, good or bad."

"But you think it was a boyfriend kind of thing?" Mason said.

"I'm thinking it was a boyfriend who didn't want to be a father," Peggy said. "A twenty-something party girl would be chasing guys, and I know she did that in later years. So if he didn't want to have a kid, she left him out of it, maybe protecting him so that I couldn't go after him. But now that she's gone, I really wonder if there's any way to find out."

"You have to try, at least," Ned said.

"Yeah, I guess. I appreciate the support, guys. I don't know what I would have done without you this past year."

"I wouldn't have had it any other way," Mason said.

"Hear, hear," Ned said. He was putting the gaskets on his canning jars one by one and sealing them.

"OK, loud noise," Peggy said, and flipped on the blender. Over the roar she said, "Mason, what the hell is this I'm hearing about you working for a church?"

Mason found it funny that her first reaction was not to the news that he'd left his office job, nor the news that he was going to try to make a living as a psychic. Los Angeles is a place where reinventing yourself meets little resistance; people tend to expect it and adapt to it with ease. Part of it was the culture of a new and rapidly evolving place, but part of it, he thought, was because it's the last stop at the far end of the continent, psychologically the end of the line. Every time there was a disaster in some other part of the country, there was a surge of new arrivals aiming to reinvent, almost as if LA was specifically set up for it.

Of more concern to Peggy was that a church was involved, as if that put Mason at some kind of risk. He waited for the blender to stop, and then explained what had happened at St. Agatha's.

"So why do you call this woman 'Miss'? I haven't called anyone 'Miss' since grade school," Peggy said. She poured the almond mush out of the blender container into a fine-mesh fabric bag that she held open with her other hand, the liquid slowly running into a bowl underneath.

"Well, she introduced herself that way. And she's older than me, so it feels appropriate. Maybe it's a Southern thing, I don't know. Lots of African American culture is Southern, like the food. She's kind of formal, and her dialect isn't really South LA; she sounds like she went to school somewhere else."

Mason drained his coffee cup and finally felt lucid enough to join in the cooking. "So I guess I'm going to have to make the cake," he said, and got up and started pulling ingredients out of the cupboards. "What kind of vinegar do I use for that apple cake you make?" he asked Ned.

"Apple cider, on the left there." Ned pulled his binder of favorite recipes off the kitchen bookshelf and flipped through until he found the one Mason needed, then set it on the counter for him.

"So who are the suspects?" Peggy asked. "Do you have any hunches yet?"

"No, but basically everyone who gets near the money is a suspect. I need to spend more time there to see if anyone seems suspicious. But the people who handle the money are Miss Cassie and the other warden, Mrs. Lewis, along with the two stewards who pass the plates during the collection, Michael and Justin. And the vicar, of course."

"Even the vicar's a suspect? That seems harsh," she said.

"I have to be objective," Mason said. "That means no one is above suspicion."

"You know, I don't like that you're going to be messing with a thief," Ned said. "It's the kind of thing you said you didn't want to do, getting involved in legal problems."

"Yeah, shouldn't the cops be the ones handling this?" Peggy said.

"I'm not going to be confronting anyone," Mason said. "I'm just going to figure out who it is and pass that information along to Miss Cassie. She'll use my input to get physical evidence of the thievery, hopefully, and then she'll call the cops."

"Even so, it concerns me," Ned said. "It's so lurid."

"Lurid would be trying to catch the thief myself, getting into a car chase or something."

"That would be quite a sight," Peggy said. "The thief roars away in a Buick and you pedal after him on your bike."

"You know, Peggy, that's a vivid and humorous

image, but there's nothing emasculating about cycling." He knew she was just teasing, but couldn't help feeling irritated.

"You know I'm kidding," she said. "Besides, if you had a car, there'd be less room on our street for me to find parking, what with all Ned's cars hogging up the garage."

"Anyway," Mason said pointedly, "it's all perfectly safe. I'll watch what happens tomorrow during the service and hopefully get some psychic vibes."

He had finished mixing the dry ingredients and the wet ingredients separately, and Ned had set out a cake pan, already oiled and dusted with flour. He was great to work with in the kitchen, always thinking ahead, Mason thought. He'd even heated the oven. Vegan cooking has its own chemistry, and one of the ways to get fluffy cake is the reaction between the dry ingredients and the vinegar in the wet ingredients. This meant the batter had to make it into the oven fairly quickly after the parts were combined.

"Ready to go," he said, and popped the pan in the oven.

Peggy said, "You know what might be fun? You could watch from the organ loft, as per your plan, and I could go undercover, on the ground, in the congregation. I'd be your eyes and ears on the floor. A mole, so to speak."

"I appreciate the offer, but I don't think it would work. You'd stand out. People would be watching you, which means you couldn't really be watching them."

"Not if I change my hair and wear work

clothes. Nobody ever recognizes me as Peggy Pregnant when I put my hair up and wear glasses."

Mason smiled. "It's not about your stage persona; it's more about the neighborhood. The congregation is almost completely African American. You'd totally stand out." Before she could pursue it any further, he said, "But there is something you could help me with."

Peggy was a Renaissance woman whose interests spanned all kinds of creative endeavors. Over the years that Mason had known her, her music had been a constant, but she had also thrown ceramics, blown glass, and sewn her own clothes. Her focus was usually serial, one pursuit replacing another. The messiest one was when she got interested in cuneiform and was mixing up batches of quick-drying plaster in the kitchen so she could recreate the effect of pressing a stylus into wet clay, the way Mesopotamian accountants had done millennia ago; he had been relieved when that one was over. In the past few years she had done some graphic design and illustration, including designing their household holiday card.

"I need a logo for my new business," Mason said. "Something cosmic, but not too light and fluffy. Cosmic but serious, you know? And it has to fit on a business card."

"Yeah, I can probably do something like that," she said. "Did you have any specific imagery in mind?"

"Not really. I thought I'd leave it to a creative expert."

"I'll see what comes to mind. Give me a day or two. I'm playing a gig tonight, but I can work on it tomorrow."

LATE IN THE DAY, after Peggy had bottled the almond milk, Ned had sealed his last jar of tomatoes and filled the pantry with them, and the cake had been set enticingly on the bar, they had a quick dinner together. They decided to have salad to let the house cool off after the day's cooking. With the screen doors open to the balcony and the front door open to the street, a bit of breeze drifted through. After they'd eaten, Mason got up to get the cake and put the plate in the middle of the table.

"Save me a slice," Peggy said, getting up. "I'll eat it later. Have you seen my baby?"

"How could you misplace that thing? It's huge," Ned said, cutting himself a slice of cake.

She was talking about her strap-on fake pregnancy, the central part of her Peggy Pregnant stage persona. She had been playing pubs and clubs around LA for years, and anyone who saw her perform more than a few times must have realized she wasn't really pregnant. But no one ever called her on it, or questioned it when they wrote about her, and Mason had never overheard anyone at one of her gigs say, "She's not really pregnant." He suspected that the music crowd and the clubgoers were afraid to say it because it might reveal something lacking in them: that they were missing the true intention of it, or not understanding Peggy's irony. Part of being hip was not being taken in or getting passionate about anything, and if you weren't sure, the best solution was not to say anything at all.

A big shift in art in her lifetime was that the creator's intent had become an important part of understanding a piece of art. This was something new; in decades past the accepted wisdom was "trust the tale, not the teller." One result was that most people now hesitated to talk about art unless they had direct knowledge of the piece. So as long as Peggy didn't explain herself, she got a pass and was accepted at face value. Her favorite tweet from a spectator at one of her performances was, "Oh my gawd this singer is 20 months pregnant I think she's going to pop on stage." She had printed it out and tacked it on the fridge with a magnet.

Sometimes she affected pangs of pain and massaged her faux belly on stage, but usually it was just a prop that created a unique visual, a very pregnant woman laboring over an acoustic guitar. Peggy Pregnant was serious and almost gloomy, unlike the real-world Peggy, who had a much more well-rounded personality and a dry sense of humor. She had confided to Mason and Ned that she found the pregnant belly at a film-industry prop house's bankruptcy sale and had worn it on stage once as a lark. People took her so much more seriously that night, she said, that she just kept wearing it, and the character evolved from there.

Ned and Mason finished eating their slices of cake, and Mason started stacking their plates. Ned reclined in his chair, looking satisfied.

"Great food," he said.

"I found it," Peggy shouted from her bedroom.

"I saw your acoustic guitar by the front door," Mason shouted back to her.

"We just call it a guitar," she said, walking back into the living room.

"No computer, no music," he said, twisting around to see her. It was an ongoing mock debate between them. He had tried to explain to her time and again that the development of synthesizers and sequencers had been the dawn of a great leap forward in human enlightenment, like Newton's physics or Pasteur's insights into germs, broadening human understanding of the world. House music was a subsequent high point, a brilliant, logical, and necessary advance in human evolution, a breakthrough that would have been hard to predict but was so essential and so right that one could only listen in awe. Peggy held that low-tech was the only way to make true music, and that any technology beyond an amplifier detracted from the art form.

Peggy had her stage outfit on: the pregnant belly, a billowy peasant maternity blouse embroidered with pink flowers, bell-bottom jeans, and clunky German-looking rattan wedges. Her hair was down, long and straight, and she wore a headband of appliqué daisies.

"How do I look?" she asked them.

"Pregnant," Mason said.

"Very pregnant," Ned said. "One might even say 1960s pregnant. How do you drive in that thing?"

"The shoes? I take them off to work the pedals."

"No, I mean the belly."

"As fast as the traffic allows, baby." She went to the door and picked up her guitar case.

"Where are you playing?" Mason asked.

"Oh, some coffeehouse in Mount Washington. Or is it Eagle Rock? I don't know, somewhere over there. I just go where Google tells me. I probably won't be home late," she said, and pushed her way out the door to the street, her guitar case bumping on the door frame.

Ned and Mason finished loading the dishwasher and sat on the sofa. Mason lay with his head in Ned's lap and his feet at the other end of the sofa, and Ned rested his arm across his chest.

"Hey, I wonder if you can get any psychic insights about Peggy's dad," Ned said.

"I thought about that today," Mason said. "I'd love to, but I'd hate to get her hopes up, especially if there are other avenues of research for her to look into first."

"But if she asks you, you'd try?"

"Of course. And I had a weird dream about music, so maybe it's connected to her," Mason said.

"So you get psychic inspiration in dreams as well?"

"I try to get information that way. It's not always clear, and it usually doesn't make much sense. But the idea is to give yourself the suggestion that you'll have a lucid dream, meaning a dream that you can kind of interact with and explore, and maybe learn something."

"That's what you were you mumbling about last night before you fell asleep."

"I was giving myself the autosuggestion to dream about the St. Agatha's business," Mason said. "You can even contact other parts of your greater self, other personalities, for example your other incarnations."

Ned said, "You mean you can talk to the person you were in a past life?"

"Not really a past life, because past and future are just illusions we experience because we're so focused in our version of reality. In broader terms, everything happens at the same time. So I could connect with some part of myself that lived in what we perceive as a hundred years ago just as easily as with someone I will be a hundred years from now."

"You realize that it's sounding kind of New Agey now, right?" Ned said.

"I guess," Mason said. "But in my mind it's not religious at all."

"OK," he said, more gently. He squeezed Mason's arm. "And so these other versions of you that you can communicate with are, what, like photocopies of you?"

"Well, the theory is that the structure of the individual is like this one massive central person that has incarnations in different times and places. Maybe it's like a bicycle wheel: the wheel is the whole person, and each spoke is a unique personality living a life somewhere. The hub is like the center that understands how it's all put together, but the spokes don't necessarily see the overall structure. You know, there might even be other fragments of your whole self living concurrently with you."

"As in other incarnations of me who live some-where else and have their own personalities and their own lives."

"Exactly."

"That is kind of a mind-blowing idea," Ned admitted, "and I must say it's not really like most religious beliefs about reincarnation. Tibetans have reincarnation, but people are supposedly reborn sequentially, to pick up where they left off the last time." He rubbed Mason's chest absentmindedly. "If that were true, if there were other versions of me out there, I'd like to meet some of them."

"Well, that's the point of connecting with them in lucid dreams."

"So for your research, what benefit is there in talking to these other versions of you?"

"We have complementary information. Among the lot of us, we exist in multiple realities that have overlapping parts. So what I experience as the St. Agatha's mystery is experienced as something else by my other selves. They might have more insight into it, which might allow me to see it from a different perspective."

"Well, maybe you can communicate with Peggy's mom's reincarnational self from the eighties, and find out who she was sleeping with."

"Not a bad idea. I think I'm probably a few years away from achieving that level of precision, though."

CUDDLING WITH NED IN bed that night before going to sleep, in the hypnagogic state Mason told

himself that he would be aware that he was dreaming. It may have worked, because in one of his
dreams he knew that he could try to change things.
He was walking down a hallway with vivid pictures
of rural landscapes on the walls. If this is a dream,
he reasoned, he should be able to pull open that
wall and walk into the landscape. He stood before
one of the images and thrust his hands into the
wall, pulling it apart. It slid open effortlessly, like a
shoji door. The moment he thought *shoji door,* the
wall took on a shoji pattern. Maybe I'm really able
to do this, he thought. He slid the shoji aside and
stepped through. On the other side was the same
kind of hallway with the same kind of landscape
images. He walked around a little, but each time he
stepped through a wall he was in the same hallway
again, which he found thoroughly annoying.

He decided to try to dissolve the dream and let
it evolve without his influence. The hallway faded.
Soon he was faced with a spinning mass, black
and formless. It gradually coalesced and flattened
into a disk. It was an old vinyl record, he realized,
floating in nothingness. It was brightly lit, and as it
spun in place, unsupported, sparkly golden threads
spiraled off from its outer rim. The threads rose
above the disc in billowing arcs, looping gracefully
around one another. It was quite beautiful, but he
was really a spectator and not influencing the way
it unfolded. And again, he thought when he woke
up, it didn't really say anything about St. Agatha's.
But he wrote it down anyway, blinking sleep out
of his eyes.

Sunday

MASON WAS ALWAYS TIRED when he had to get up early, and this morning he was even more exhausted than usual. Trying to manipulate his dreams must have worn him out, he thought. If he had to work in both waking life and in the dream state, he'd never get any rest. He gulped down as much espresso as he could stomach, gnawed on a peach and some strawberries, and stumbled into his suit. It was an ill-fitting gray catchall for weddings and funerals that he would tart up with a colorful necktie for happy events and a dark one for somber things.

Ned came into the bedroom. "Hiya, toots. Are

you late?" he asked.

"Not yet, but it's going to be close. Do I look OK in the suit? I wish I had a fedora to go with it."

"What you need is a purple satin turban with a four-hundred-carat fake ruby on the front."

"What? Why?"

"You know, like a vaudeville psychic."

"Oh. Funny." He managed a wan smile, kissed Ned on the cheek, and went out the front door to the street. He hustled down the hill to the metro as quickly as he could on foot. He couldn't bring himself to cycle in a suit; the thought of it gave him visions of flailing wool and polyester snarled in the chain and gears, with him flying over the handlebars like a living Robert Longo charcoal. Even in the early morning, before the heat had really built up, the trouser legs felt clingy and itchy, and no matter how often he adjusted his necktie it felt like it was choking him. He wondered if the sweat would percolate through his suit jacket in the places where the weight of his backpack was pressing on it.

Thirty minutes on the metro gave him a chance to cool off. Unlike with cycling, there was no way to make the train move any faster, so once he was on board he was usually able to let go of the rush toward the goal and be reflective. The train came above ground, and he watched the city slide by. It was Sunday, so lots of people were out with their families rather than racing to work. He realized that he felt happy to be free of his job, to be out so early and doing other things. It felt a bit weird not to have a routine waiting for him on Monday, but under that he felt happy, like the sky had brightened.

He worked up a sweat again walking from the metro station to St. Agatha's kitchen door. He glanced at his phone and was relieved to see it was just eight o'clock.

"Right on time," Miss Cassie said as he pulled the door open.

"Yes, uh, no traffic at this hour. I parked around the corner."

"Let's get you installed upstairs," she said. "I'm afraid it's going to get pretty warm up there, especially when hundreds of people are packed into the pews. But I'll crank the air-conditioning as high as I dare. I hope the heat won't interfere with your psychic reception." She raised her eyebrows and looked at him over her glasses.

He wasn't sure if she was joking or not, but the only thing he was really afraid of was the combination of the heat and eighteenth-century hymns putting him to sleep.

She climbed ahead of him up to the organ loft, where he saw she had set out a couple of kneeler cushions for him to sit on, along with a bottle of water.

"This looks comfortable," Mason said.

"Now, as soon as you see the minister leave the chancel, you should head downstairs. Nobody will be in the hall yet. I'll leave the door to the offices unlocked, and you can meet me in there. Mrs. Lewis will bring the collection plates in right after the minister steps away from them."

"Does she know that I'll be there?" he asked.

"Not yet, but don't worry about her. I'll explain it all to her when she gets there." With that she climbed back down the stairs and closed the door at the bottom.

It was already warm in the loft, and he took off his suit jacket, hanging it on one of the shorter organ pipes. He wondered if it would interfere with the sound, and thought about moving it, but he had enough trouble keeping the thing from looking disheveled, and putting it on the floor would only make it worse, so he decided to leave it. His backpack, however, could stay on the floor. It was still two hours until the service would start. Surely a few minutes' sleep wouldn't hurt? He was afraid of missing something, though, and in any case there wasn't enough room to stretch out. He got as comfortable as he could on the kneeler cushions. He pulled out his phone to put it in silent mode, and then he texted Ned, "Bored. Talk to me." But he didn't answer.

Things started to pick up around 9:30. Mason sat cross-legged in the dimness, looking through the railing at the people below. He got a good look at the vicar, who didn't move very fast, which made Mason think he probably wasn't capable of the sleight of hand required to steal from the collection plates in front of hundreds of his parishioners. He recognized both collection stewards, Michael and Justin, when they came in. Neither of them looked especially shady. At one point Michael crossed in front of the altar carrying the collection plates.

Why hadn't he seen those in the church's safe? Perhaps they were too big to fit, or they didn't have any value and could be left out on a shelf. They looked like simple polished bronze, a bowl with a wide brim, like a soup plate. Why hadn't he thought to do psychometry on them on Friday? Mason had the feeling he often had when he went to the grocery store without a shopping list—like he knew he was missing something, but he wasn't sure what. He would have to read those plates when he went down to the office, he thought.

He saw the demure organist take her seat at the desk with the organ keyboard, behind the pulpit. Sitting bolt upright, she fired up the great beast behind Mason with the press of a button. It startled him at first with an electric snap, and then it settled into a low hum and a continuous wheezing. The organist started to play somber background music to welcome the people who slowly filled the pews, and lucky for him, sitting right next to the pipes, it was loud but not deafening.

The church was packed by the time the service started, a sea of big hats on the women and the men in dark jackets or white shirts, all wearing neckties. Mason tried to stay aware of his inner senses. It was a bit like meditating with his eyes open: he tried to reduce the chatter in his mind and the visual information to a narrow stream, allowing enough empty space for psychic inspiration.

The vicar performed the service in a thin, reedy voice with an unmistakable southern-hemisphere lilt. Mason purposefully tuned out the sermon to concentrate on his inner channels. The hymns weren't all the same lifeless two-hundred-year-old corpses that he remembered from his youth. "That's why the English went out and took over forty percent of the planet," his father had once said. "At home they had bad weather, bad food, and those damn hymns." St. Agatha's had some modern and fairly upbeat and animated hymns, but maintained a few of the somber and dry old ones:

> When the day of toil is done,
> When the race of life is run,
> Father, grant thy wearied one
> Rest for evermore.

Jesus H. Christ, Mason thought, put us out of our misery now.

He perked up when the Eucharist was being offered. People lined up and milled around, and eventually everyone who wanted to had knelt for the bread and wine. People seemed to be enlivened, perhaps from the Eucharist itself, or from having a little booze, or more likely from the thought that it was almost over. The collection plates were passed down the pews from the aisle, where the stewards stood and waited for them to be passed back. It would have been impossible for anyone to remove anything from the plate as it was passed along, he thought, with so many eyes on them. Michael and Justin didn't appear to lift anything from the plates either, although he didn't always have a clear view of them. So many people were watching them, though, it seemed unlikely.

The vicar offered the collection plates to God, covered them with a cloth, and a moment later dismissed the congregation and opened the gate in the communion rail. Mason stood up quickly, but his left leg had fallen asleep; he stumbled backward but caught his balance on the organ cabinet. He pulled on his suit jacket to cover at least part of his sweat-stained shirt, slung his backpack over one shoulder, and stumbled down the stairs as quietly as he could. Someone was clattering around in the kitchen. He gently pushed the door to the hall open a couple of inches and peered through the gap. The lights were on in the hall, but no one was inside yet, as Miss Cassie had predicted. He shifted his weight without considering his impaired leg and lost his balance, falling off the last step and landing in a sprawl on the floor of the hall. He looked around and dragged himself up; no one had seen him. He grabbed his backpack from the floor and hobbled quickly along the side of the hall, running his palm along the wall to keep his balance, his leg throbbing.

Miss Cassie was there in the office, behind the desk, and the collection plates sat in front of her. A well-dressed woman, probably in her late fifties, stood in front of the desk; Mason knew it must be Mrs. Lewis. She turned around as he limped in, a look of surprise on her face. He stood a few feet back from the corner of the desk, trying to look nonchalant and not sweaty as he stooped to massage his thigh.

"Hello," Mason said, and attempted a disarming grin. He had to fight the urge to say "I love your hat"—it was a spectacular and distracting maroon swirl of fabric and feathers that managed to be elegant despite its complexity.

"Betty," Miss Cassie said, "this is Mason Braithwaite. Mason, meet Betty Lewis. He's here to help us figure out why the money has been going missing."

"Oh," she said, looking even more surprised. "Are you with the police?"

"No, no, I'm not. I'm a …" he hesitated when Miss Cassie almost imperceptibly shook her head. Obviously not everyone would be comfortable bringing a psychic into the church. "I'm an investigator."

"Oh, I see." She smiled. "I guess it's typecasting of me to assume you're a policeman because you're white."

"Have you taken a good look at the police lately?" Miss Cassie asked. "It's not 1992 anymore, honey. They come in every color of the rainbow now. And they've got women in there too."

"Of course, of course. I should know better. So, what have you found out?" she asked, turning back to Mason.

"I can't really comment yet, ma'am," he said, trying to sound authoritative. "But I'm here to observe the count of the collection. Just pretend I'm not here."

Her eyebrows rose, and she turned to look at Miss Cassie, who nodded. Mrs. Lewis said nothing but sat down and carefully emptied the collection plates onto the desktop, glancing back at

Mason once, wide-eyed, before getting to work. Mason realized she must have figured out that she could be under suspicion as much as anyone else. There was a lot of money, he thought, as it tumbled onto the desk. He could see why a thief would be tempted. A moment later the door from the church opened, and one of the collection stewards came in. When he saw Mason, he looked startled, but didn't acknowledge him. It was Michael, Mason remembered from the photos in the files.

"I'll put those collection plates away for you," Michael said to Miss Cassie. He glanced at Mason again. Miss Cassie handed Michael the plates, and he went through the offices into the church hall, closing the door behind him. It struck Mason as a little suspicious, but he couldn't claim that to be a psychic inspiration.

"Where do those get stored?" Mason asked.

"The collection plates? I think he keeps them in a cupboard at the back of the hall," Miss Cassie said.

"Is it his job to do that?"

"Well, he is the collection steward, or one of them. So, yes, it's his job," she said.

"Why doesn't he store them here in the office?" Mason said.

"I don't like where this is going," Mrs. Lewis said. "Michael's a good man. His family has been involved with our sister parish for decades."

"But not with this church?" Mason asked.

"No, in San Diego."

"Still, I'd like to have a look at those plates. You

know, to examine them," Mason said, giving Miss Cassie a meaningful look, and making air quotes with his fingers when he said the word *examine.*

"I get it," Miss Cassie said, not quite impatiently, and stood up. "I'll go get them."

While she was gone, Mrs. Lewis turned to look at Mason. He smiled politely but found the situation unnerving. "I love your hat," he blurted out.

"Do you know why women in black churches wear such elaborate hats?" she said.

"I have no idea."

"Back before the civil rights movement, when we were only able to get menial jobs, we had to wear the uniform of a cook or a cleaner six days a week. Sunday was the only time to get fancy and express our own fashion. And the tradition continues today."

"I'm certainly glad things have changed since then."

"Me too," she said. Her eyes narrowed. "So who do you work for as an investigator?"

"Oh, I'm self-employed," he said, and before he had to say any more, Miss Cassie was back, plates in hand.

"That was a bit odd," she said.

"What do you mean?" Mrs. Lewis said.

"Michael has been storing these in the cleaning cupboard. I had to ask him where they were; he had them in a box up on a high shelf."

"I suppose he doesn't want them to get stolen," she said.

"Then why not keep them in here?" Mason

said. "There's a safe, and locking file cabinets." They both looked at him but didn't have an answer. "May I?" he said, and held out his hand. Miss Cassie handed them over. "I'm going to sit at the desk in the next office and examine these," Mason said. "I'll let you get on with counting the take."

"We're not a casino, dear," Mrs. Lewis said gently. "Casinos have a take. At church it's called the offering."

"I see. Of course," he said, and quickly stepped into the other office before she could see him blush.

He sat behind the desk and put the plates on it, side by side. They were brass, surprisingly heavy for their size, maybe twelve inches across. The bowl was about eight inches across and had a green felt circle in the bottom; the rest of the width was the broad flat rim. The two plates were similar, though not identical; one was perhaps newer. He sat back in the chair and closed his eyes. When he had sufficiently suppressed the chatter and random background thoughts—which took a few minutes because of the noise of the congregants talking and laughing over coffee and cakes in the hall next door, and some knucklehead laying on a car horn outside—he reached for one of the plates.

With his eyes closed he didn't get a good grip on it, and had to snatch at it to prevent it from falling. As he grabbed it he felt the rim slide slightly against the lower part of the bowl. He inspected it, and sure enough, with a little pressure he could make the rim rotate. He tried the other bowl, but it was a single solid piece of brass and wouldn't budge.

He played with the moving part for a minute, and realized that a small gap was opening up along the side of the bowl. It was just an eighth of an inch wide, but plenty big enough to stuff paper money or tithing envelopes into. When he rotated it more, the gap closed up again and became invisible. He picked at the edge of the green felt inlay in the bottom, and it popped off in one solid piece; the felt was glued to a wooden disk. When put back in place, the disk looked no different than the one in the other plate, but it left a shallow space that could also easily hide a wad of cash and tithing envelopes. The felt on the other plate was glued directly onto the brass, immovable.

"Ladies," he called to the next office, "you're going to want to see this."

"THAT BASTARD," MISS CASSIE spat after Mason had demonstrated the secret compartment in the plate. "It has to be Michael. He's the one who took charge of these plates and hid them every week."

"Now, Cassie, you're in a church," Mrs. Lewis said, but it was the gentlest of admonitions.

"See, here's the reason he was stealing envelopes as well as cash," Mason said, rotating the plate's rim. "When you twist the mechanism, you can slide whatever's under your hand into the compartment with your thumb, but you can't be selective about it. He had to be subtle because he was doing it in front of everybody."

"Let's get him," Miss Cassie said, and yanked open the door to the hall. Mason felt a surge of fear. What if Michael carried a knife or something? This was exactly what Ned had warned him about. But he compelled himself to follow Mrs. Lewis into the crowd of people in the hall, close on the heels of Miss Cassie, who walked around the large room and discreetly asked a few people if they'd seen Michael. Mrs. Lewis held back and followed her at a distance. Mason scanned the room and saw the other collection steward, Justin, but not Michael.

More than a few people did a double-take when they saw Mason craning to see over the crowd. Following Miss Cassie, he bumped into the vicar, although it took a moment to recognize him out of his cassock. He smiled benevolently, but Mason saw that he was also perplexed by the tall redhead. Miss Cassie had definitely kept the whole inquiry quiet. Eventually someone pointed her to the big double doors at the back of the hall, which were propped open. The three of them walked toward the doors, and Mason saw that they opened to the parking lot.

A young man in a bow tie stepped inside. "What happened to Michael?" he asked the women.

"Where is he?" Miss Cassie demanded.

"Last I saw him, he was running up Rosewood. He was trying to get his car out of the parking lot, but it's really crowded and somebody had blocked him in. He kind of freaked out, and then he took off running. He didn't even close his car door."

"OK," she said. "Could you lock up his car? Bring me the keys, if they're still there. And please don't mention this to anyone else in the hall."

He looked puzzled but deferred to Miss Cassie. "Yes, ma'am."

"Should we go after him?" Mason asked.

"There's no way we'll find him now. Come on," she said quietly, glancing around at the people in the hall. Her initial flash of anger seemed to have faded, her focus shifting to her community. A few of the congregants looked on curiously as they walked back through the hall, but most of them were engaged in fellowship and hadn't noticed anything odd. The three of them went back into the office, and Miss Cassie closed the door.

"Running off like that is as good as an admission of guilt," Mason said.

"Perhaps it's just as well that we didn't get a chance to confront him," Mrs. Lewis said. "It would have been an awful scene. He won't dare show his face around here again. Now, shall we call the police?"

"Not now. We don't need any more fuss here today," Miss Cassie said, shaking her head. She looked almost relieved as she sank into her chair. Mrs. Lewis and Mason sat down too, the three of them around the desk again, with the collection plates sitting in the middle of it. "I'll go to the station tomorrow with this doctored plate and a photo of him and whatever other information we have." She picked up the plate and massaged its mechanism open and closed again. "I just don't understand how we could have been so wrong about him. The parish in San Diego had nothing but good things to say about him."

"Earning your trust is how con artists work. How long has he been here?" Mason asked.

"At least a year, possibly longer. Which means it was a long-term project," Mrs. Lewis said. "Stealing the tithing envelopes was probably lucrative too, because you can sell bank account numbers if you have a name and address attached. Checks are ideal for identity theft because they have all that information written right on them."

Mason nodded. "How much do you think he got?"

"Hundreds of dollars a week, plus the checks to sell," Mrs. Lewis said.

"Well, I guess I was right to hire you. You figured it out," Miss Cassie said.

Despite the fact that he hadn't really done it using his psychic abilities, he knew she was right. And even without psychic inspiration, Mason was happy with the success. Part of it—confronting the criminal—was terrifying to him, and Miss Cassie was braver than him on that front. But mostly this felt really good, and it felt right, and it made him think he might be able to make a go of it.

"I must say, you're good at what you do," Mrs. Lewis said. "We've been tearing our hair out, and you figured it out in one day. What made you decide to examine the plates?"

"I guess it seemed like the next logical step."

"Maybe it was divine inspiration?" Miss Cassie said, and smiled.

"Or maybe dumb luck," he said.

"You should have him look for Sherri," Mrs. Lewis said.

Miss Cassie's face clouded. "Absolutely not."

"You must admit you're as curious as I am, Cassie. And this young man is a talented investigator. Are you actually a PI, dear," she asked him, "or is it called something else?"

He said, "No, I'm—" but Miss Cassie cut in.

"Sherri left of her own volition, and we don't need to stir that up. She knows my number if she wants to talk to me."

"Sherri is your daughter?" Mason asked.

"Yes," Mrs. Lewis said, looking at Miss Cassie and hesitating before she continued. "She was always a troubled girl. After high school she worked here at the church off and on, because we thought it would give her some stability. But I'm not so sure that she just up and left. In my mind it was more like she disappeared."

"Really?" Mason said. "Did you go to the police?"

"Of course not," Miss Cassie said. "She had been threatening to move out for weeks, and I was encouraging her to go. When she finally did, I never heard from her again. But that was her choice." She sighed. "We never really got along."

"How long ago was that?" Mason asked.

"Years. Maybe three years."

"More like four," Mrs. Lewis said. "No one else has heard from her since then either, and she knew a lot of people in the congregation. And then there's the credit reports."

"What credit reports?" Mason said.

"Sherri's," Mrs. Lewis said. "All the activity just stopped after she disappeared. No cell phone contract, no credit cards, no landlords. I feared the worst."

"When did you run her credit?" Mason asked.

"I've done it a couple of times," Miss Cassie said. "Most recently about six months ago. It doesn't mean that she's dead; it just means she isn't using the identity she was born with anymore. That would be very like Sherri."

"It sounds kind of devious and illegal, though," he said.

"Again, that's Sherri."

"But still, it all stopped at the same time, when she left," Mrs. Lewis said.

"Did she take her stuff with her, like her clothes?" Mason asked.

"Yes, of course."

"Did you talk to her friends, or anything like that?" he asked. He hesitated to pull his notepad out of his backpack, but did it anyway. Miss Cassie frowned as he started writing but continued her story.

"She didn't really have any close friends, at least not that I knew of," she said. "She only spent time with people who could benefit her."

"She was something of a material girl," Mrs. Lewis said in a quieter voice, leaning toward him, as if someone might overhear.

"What do you mean?" he asked.

"She was a chiseler," Miss Cassie said. "There

was never enough money. No matter what I gave her, or what job she got, it was always beneath her."

"You said you didn't get along with her. What did you fight about?" he asked.

"That's none of your business," Miss Cassie said, her face reddening.

"Everything," Mrs. Lewis said.

"You know, I could look into it," he said. "If you have a piece of jewelry, or a key that she carried with her, I could do a reading."

Mrs. Lewis looked mystified, but said to Miss Cassie, "It couldn't hurt to have him look into it. And wouldn't you like to know whether she's dead or alive?"

"I couldn't care less," Miss Cassie said, throwing her hands in the air.

"Actually, you do care, or you wouldn't be so upset about it," Mrs. Lewis said. "And if you were completely disinterested, you wouldn't have run that credit check on her six months ago."

Miss Cassie pressed her lips together and looked from her to Mason. "If you really feel compelled, go ahead. But I'm not going to pay you to do it."

"Oh, I'll pay you," Mrs. Lewis said. "I want to know if Sherri's OK, and what she's up to."

"Let's not worry about money until I do some preliminary research," Mason said.

"Fine," Miss Cassie said. "But not here, not now. I need to go back into that hall with our congregation and feign some normalcy."

"You're not going to tell people about the theft?" Mason asked.

"Not until Michael is sitting in a jail cell."

"Although you will have to explain who the man in the rumpled suit is," said Mrs. Lewis, smiling at Mason. It took him a second to realize she was talking about him. "You know, I have photos of Sherri taken when she was working with the church," she said. "Why don't you drop by my house before you go? I'm right around the corner."

"Sure," Mason said.

It seemed like he had scored another job, he thought, and while it was a bit befuddling to be shifting focus so quickly, it felt like a good opportunity. Mrs. Lewis had agreed to pay him before even asking what it would cost her, so she must have the means. And visiting her house without Miss Cassie would give him a chance to get more details on why Miss Cassie had fallen out with her daughter, which seemed almost as interesting as the job itself.

"Let's slip out through the nave and the front door, then," she said. "Everyone's in the hall now. Cassie, you'll have your hands full with damage control. There are going to be a lot of questions. Are you sure you don't need help?"

"I'm fine. Go," she said. "This will all come out eventually, but not today. Mason, my office is downtown, at Fifth and Orchard, in the Primavera Building. It's very convenient to the metro. Can you come by tomorrow afternoon around one? We'll talk about the logistics of you taking on this research project."

"I can do that," he said. But how did she know

he took the metro? he wondered.

He and Mrs. Lewis exited St. Agatha's unseen through the main door, leaving Miss Cassie to explain the fuss in the parking lot and Mason's incongruous presence.

Mrs. Lewis's house really was right around the corner, just a couple of blocks away. On the walk over she chatted about the neighborhood, neighbors' gardens, and the weather. Her house was a huge Spanish-style two-story, probably dating to the 1930s, and still the nicest house on the block.

"Such lovely roses," Mason said as they walked up the front path.

"I like nice things," she said, and smiled.

"How do you get them to bloom so profusely?"

"I hired a good gardener." She opened the front door with her key and pushed her way inside. "Come on in," she said, and waved him into the sitting room, just off the foyer. "I'll be right back." High wainscoting and dark striped wallpaper gave it a Victorian look, and the furniture was an eclectic assortment of antique and modern. It was immaculately clean and full of knickknacks, mostly framed photos and little tchotchkes, the kind of stuff that takes a lifetime to accumulate. Mason stood and looked out the window at the tree-lined street, thinking he should wait for her to return before he sat down.

As if reading his mind, she called from another part of the house, "Sit down, and make yourself comfortable." He picked an elegant wing chair that faced the doorway rather than the window. A moment later she called, "Actually, dear, could you come in here for a moment? I can't carry all this." He got up again and walked down the hall to find her, minus her elaborate hat, in the gleaming kitchen at the back of the house. It had a hexagonal-tiled floor and lovely retro glass-fronted cupboards. The only contemporary fixture was the lighting.

"Is this all original?" he asked, gesturing to the cabinets.

"Those are rebuilt, but based on what was there before. They're much bigger than the originals; I don't think people had as many dishes back then. The floor is a re-creation as well. Kitchens don't usually hold up so well after eighty years, but I loved this one, so I had it redone with the same look. And see what's under here," she said, opening a pair of cabinet doors under the countertop to reveal the front of a dishwasher.

"You're a visionary," Mason said. "I wish more people had the same good sense."

"Thank you. But it certainly wasn't cheap."

"Look at this," Mason said, walking over to the side counter where a stylish fire engine–red mixer perched beside a more prosaic coffeemaker. "My partner has been coveting this exact model for ages. Sometimes he drives us by the cooking store just to drool over it, even when it's not on the way home."

"As I said, I like nice things," she said.

"The design of this machine hasn't changed since this house was new, so it looks perfect here."

She picked up two tall glasses from the counter. "Lemonade," she said, handing him one.

"Great," he said, and took the glass. "It certainly was hot in that organ loft."

"Is that where you were?" Her eyes grew wide. "It must have been a hundred degrees up there." She picked up a plate of cookies and walked back down the hall to the front room. "Cassie certainly had some tricks up her sleeve. But I guess it was for the best; you really earned your pay today."

He decided he'd let Miss Cassie fill her in on what he'd been doing, and filter out the psychic part, as he suspected she would. He waited until she sat, on the settee facing the wing chair, before he sat down. She put the plate of cookies on the little table beside him. In one long gulp he drank as much of the lemonade as he could without appearing piggy. In a second he was glad he hadn't drunk more; it was so sweet it made his teeth ache.

"Mmm," he said appreciatively, and set the glass down carefully on a coaster on the side table, struggling not to wince. He wondered fleetingly whether so much sugar might actually be able to induce diabetes in one dose. No way was he going to try one of those cookies.

"Now, I said I had photos for you, but that was a little bit of subterfuge. I really wanted to tell you more about Sherri."

"OK," he said. "So what happened between them to make Miss Cassie so upset?" He pulled his notepad and pen out of his backpack.

"Oh, they never got along. As an objective outsider, I can say that Cassie had completely unrealistic expectations of that girl. She had to behave perfectly as a child, so I suppose that may be why Sherri rebelled later on. She was supposed to go to USC, and even got a scholarship of some kind, but then she did something to mess that up. I wasn't party to all the details, but at the time I remember thinking it was self-sabotage. Do you have children?"

"No."

"Well, troubled kids often become troubled kids during puberty, but Sherri was already extremely intense before that. One of those kids with a lot of nervous energy, and you're never sure how it's going to spill out."

He scribbled "troubled kid" and "nervous energy" on his pad, and then looked up. "You said she was materialistic?"

"Indeed. She would take advantage of people, especially boys, until they figured it out. It wasn't really that she was trampy, but she knew how to work them to get what she wanted. I think she probably got quite good at it, and perhaps that's why she left; she found a better long-term meal ticket than her mother. Or worse, she grifted the wrong person and wound up in a shallow grave out in the desert, fifty miles from nowhere."

Mason frowned. "Do you think that's likely? Miss Cassie said they had talked about her leaving, and that it didn't really come as a surprise."

"The part that was suspicious to me was that she dropped right off the map, so to speak, with no trace of any financial activity. These days that's an easy way to keep track of people." She leaned forward and spoke more softly. "I'm not asking you to bring her home, but I would like to know, one way or the other."

"I'll find out what I can," he said. "It's an interesting case, and bizarre to me that no one has tried to locate her before now."

"Well, as you said, it wasn't unexpected that she left, and she did take her things with her. She and I weren't really close, but I kept expecting to hear something, maybe not me personally, but through someone in the community. And then the weeks become years."

"I guess Miss Cassie will have a photo or two and more details. Is there anything you can remember about where she might have gone, or people she was spending time with before she disappeared?"

She looked at the carpet for a moment. She told him about some of the local boys Sherri had dated, and people she had worked with at St. Agatha's. Mostly she knew only superficial details of Sherri's life; nothing she had to offer struck Mason as especially significant. He realized that she had probably wanted to assess him apart from Miss Cassie, and to impress on him what she wanted.

He listened politely, writing down the highlights, and when she had run out of details, he stuffed his notepad into his backpack and said, "Well, thank you for the lemonade. I'll let you know when I have a better idea of whether I'm going to be able to find anything."

"Of course. But I'd like to get an idea of what your rates are before we get any farther along."

"I usually get five hundred a day plus expenses," he said. It wasn't really a lie, he reasoned, as that was what he planned to get paid eventually, and he had to start somewhere.

"I'm sure that's fine, but maybe you should run the expenses past me as they come up. And just let Cassie know how you're going to proceed after you see her tomorrow, and she'll keep me informed."

She saw him to the door, and he waved good-bye when he reached the sidewalk. He couldn't believe that she was unfazed by his salary request, considering how Miss Cassie had reacted to the same numbers. And of the two of them it seemed like Miss Cassie was the one in charge. But it might not even matter; he had no idea how he could find out anything concrete about the missing Sherri Millar. The place to start would be to do a reading of a piece of her jewelry, which he hoped Miss Cassie would have. He had to wait for that to happen before he decided it was hopeless, he reminded himself. If he expected other people to believe he was psychic, it was only reasonable that he believe it himself. It was possible that something as macabre as what Mrs. Lewis had suggested could have befallen Sherri, but it seemed unlikely, based on what they'd said about her leaving, so Mason decided to work on the assumption that she was alive.

He walked a block out of his way so that he wouldn't pass St. Agatha's parking lot; he'd been visible enough there today, he thought. Walking up a long block of apartment buildings, he saw a woman sitting out on her front steps, watching him carefully as he came up the street. "How're you?" he called to her, and nodded.

"I don't know you," she shouted at him, indignant.

"You're right," he said, surprised, and quickened his pace. Clearly not everyone in the neighborhood was as high-fructose as Mrs. Lewis.

Before heading back toward the metro, he stopped at the coffee joint in the neighborhood square. He scarfed down a bagel along with a triple espresso; it had been a long morning. The young woman working the counter remembered him from Friday.

"Do you live around here?" she asked.

"No, but I've been working in the neighborhood," Mason said.

She nodded but didn't respond. She was practically dancing to the upbeat electronic music as she prepared his coffee and made change.

"This sounds like *Metro Grooves*," he said.

"Yes, it's last night's show, from the Web." She smiled, bobbing and gyrating unself-consciously. "I love this guy. I used to listen to it online too when I worked in an office."

"Isn't it fun?"

"Indeed it is."

It was a brief exchange, but he was happy to be able to talk to a stranger in the neighborhood without getting verbally assaulted.

"WHAT I DON'T GET is how they could have overlooked the trick collection plate for a whole year, and you just walk in there one day and figure it out. It's pretty amazing," Ned said over dinner. He had made butter beans over rice, doused with his sage gravy. It was delicious; Peggy was missing out, Mason thought.

"I just think they didn't know where to look. I didn't know either, but I found out. So she was right to hire me."

"But you can't really say that psychic power played a big part in finding the solution."

"No," Mason said, "but then I can't say that it didn't play a part. I might have been given information subconsciously. That's the thing with psychic power: it's hard to pin down."

"Well, however you did it, I'm happy for you. It didn't take you long to show that you might be able to pull it off, this whole new career thing. When do you get paid?"

"When the police catch the guy. We agreed that I'd get a bonus if someone gets charged with a crime."

"How cool is that," Ned said, and squeezed his arm. "And you got another gig out of it too. How are you going to look for this woman's daughter? With old-fashioned research?"

"You know I love the library," Mason said. "I'll definitely go down there and see what I can find out. That might lead me to some psychic insights, although I'm not sure I'll be able to come up with anything."

"Don't be so sure. You were confident about helping St. Agatha's, and you cracked that one in a couple of days. Just because Miss Cassie's not confident in you doesn't mean you won't do just fine with this one too."

"Thank you," Mason said, and looked at him carefully. "Damn, you've certainly adapted to my new career path quickly."

"Well, it's your new career, and it's our new reality, so I'm working to accept it. And hey, you're already making money. I went to a meeting too, which helps a lot with the acceptance part, to be reminded of the power of that. I want to love you the way you are, without putting my own stuff on you, my expectations or demands or whatever. And we don't necessarily have to have the same frame of reference, to believe the same stuff."

"That works for me," Mason said, and leaned over to kiss him on the neck.

"I'm still not buying that ESP exists. It's too much like religion, the leap of faith."

"I guess complete acceptance would be too much to expect," Mason said. "But as long as you can handle my changes without getting upset, I'm happy."

"I think people do it often these days, right, switch careers and reinvent, especially with the messed-up economy, and with technology changing so quickly," Ned said. "Gilbert has had more careers than I can count. So I think I need to catch up with the pace of change in the world."

"Didn't Gilbert leave his last job because he thought the company had implanted him with a tracking device?" Mason asked.

"Well, he did have that weird lump on his arm. He's definitely happier not working there, regardless."

"I know exactly how that feels." It might have been because of the rapid pace of events over the last few days, but his life in gossip publishing seemed to be receding quickly. "So where's Peggy?"

"She was going to spend the day with that guy she's seeing, the young one."

"You mean Van? He's not that young."

"Younger than her. They were going downtown to the library—you must be on the same wavelength as her. She wanted to do a records search to see if there's anything about her mother that might tell her something about her father. But her mother wasn't a public figure, so I wonder how likely it is that she'll find anything about her in the newspapers."

"There are other resources besides the newspapers," Mason said. "A librarian would have access to more stuff, other databases. Even an old phone book might provide a clue, if she could identify someone else living with her mom, for example. They used to publish cross-reference phone books back then so you could look up people by an address or by a phone number. It's a place to start, anyway."

DRIFTING OFF TO SLEEP that night, Mason repeated to himself several times the suggestion that he'd have a lucid dream and astrally project to find out where Sherri was. It was an ambitious goal, as he'd never had much luck with projecting his consciousness away from his body, but maybe if he did well with the lucid dreaming, it would happen organically.

He became aware in his dreams that he was dreaming. He seemed to be in the tunnels under a stadium or a coliseum, with other people milling around. He willed himself to project above the stadium so that he could see it, and soon he started to float off the ground. He rose a little higher and turned to look at himself below, seemingly only six or eight feet away. He had a sudden rush of fear and panic. He didn't want to be disconnected from his body, even his dream body; what if he couldn't get back into it? In a flash he snapped back to the ground. After that he knew he had lost the sense of awareness that he was dreaming. When he woke up he pulled out his notepad and wrote "Under a stadium. Floated out of body. Terrifying. Fell back into body right away." It didn't look like much on paper, he thought, even though it had felt like a lot of work. But maybe he was making some progress with the technique.

Monday

Miss Cassie was right, Mason realized: the Primavera Building was just across the street from the entrance to the metro. It was a striking tower dating probably to the 1930s, he estimated, based on the soaring art deco style, complete with zigzag details a few feet above eye level. He would have walked by it before, but he'd never stopped to look at it closely.

He phoned Miss Cassie when he came up the stairs from the train, and she gave him her office number. The building's lobby was equally sensational, with murals stretching to the twenty-foot ceiling and a zigzag marble floor, the elevators with luxe dark mahogany paneling. Off the elevator and down the hall, a sign tacked on her office door read "Come in." He pulled it open, and saw that there were no art deco details here; instead it was a very modern space, perhaps eight hundred square feet, with bare concrete floors and ceilings and huge windows on two sides. There was only one interior wall, with an open doorway probably leading to a washroom or storage, he thought. It was sparsely furnished, with only one desk, a lot of bookshelves, and a sitting area with a sofa and chairs.

"Hello," Miss Cassie said, walking around her desk and giving him a feminine handshake. He had almost overlooked her as he took in the dramatic space.

"Great place," he said. "What is it exactly that you do?"

"I'm a psychologist. I guess we never really talked about that. Do you like the space? It's a bit echoey, but the carpeting around this end of it helps." Beyond her desk there was a thick rug, almost the same color as the concrete floor, under the sofa and chairs.

"It's stunning. The deco outside is glammy too."

"Not all the floors have been rehabbed, but they do a pretty good job with maintaining the exterior. The only problem is parking. It was built in the 1930s when nobody really had a car. I have to park under Pershing Square." She gestured to the sofa, and Mason sat down. She took one of the adjacent easy chairs.

"So did you go to the police today?" he asked.

"This very morning. I made a pretty comprehensive statement, and they put a burglary detective on it. I didn't mention the psychic-power element of the whole thing, only that you'd found the altered collection plate, which I left with them. I gave her your name and number, but I doubt that she'll need to talk to you directly."

"Whatever's necessary."

"I told her that you were a contract worker for the church administration looking into personnel issues, which is absolutely true, but not mentioning the psychic component means that if this story hits the media—which I really hope it won't—it won't sound any more bizarre than it has to."

He nodded. "That makes perfect sense to me." He got the feeling that she wanted to be sure he wasn't going to take the story to the media himself. "Personally, I'd rather not have to talk to the police or the media, and of course I'm going to treat this as confidential. You're my client, so it's your show, and I'll handle it as you see fit."

"Good," she said, and Mason could see relief in her expression. "I know we talked about confidentiality, but I wanted to reiterate it."

"If they arrest him and charge him, though, that's public record, so it'll hit the media regardless."

"We'll deal with that when it comes up. Of course, you'd have to tell this detective the truth, if she wants to interview you, but I think it's straightforward enough that she won't need to. Her priority now is to talk to Michael."

"Let's hope they can track him down. It sounds

like he was moving pretty fast on Sunday. He must have known we were on to him."

"I think he knew the jig was up when I asked him to give me the collection plates two minutes after he'd taken them to squirrel them away," she said. "He gave them to me, but by the time I handed them to you, he was gone. Do you remember all the honking? That was him trying to get out of the parking lot. He knew we were about to figure it out."

"An innocent man wouldn't have run away," he said. "So, about getting paid, do you want me to invoice you or something?"

"No, I don't think that'll be necessary. Can we wait a week or so to see if they're able to find Michael? If they recover any of our money, I want to turn some of it into a bonus for you. And it's not a delay tactic; you will get paid."

"I'm not worried. I'm just happy that I was able to help."

"Now, this business about my daughter." She squared her shoulders, folded her hands in front of her, and looked aside for a moment as if gathering her thoughts. "The suggestion that she might be dead is sheer melodrama. I'm not psychic, but I'm certain that she's alive and well. That said, I really don't need to know where she is, or what she's doing, although I am a little curious. I still feel strongly about her, I have to admit that. Betty was right to call me on it yesterday. I guess it's obvious that I'm reacting emotionally, so I can't really claim to be detached from Sherri or indifferent about her."

"I don't see how you could be, no matter how long it's been."

"True. So perhaps a little bit of news won't be a bad thing. And Betty harps on the matter now and then, so maybe the simple act of looking into it will put her mind at ease."

"I'll do what I can, Miss Cassie."

"And I have to tell you, based on what I saw at church on Sunday, I know you're not really psychic. I suspect that such things are possible, these psychic insights, but I didn't see it in you. Your work was admirable, but it had nothing to do with the supernatural, and everything to do with rational real-world thinking. So is the psychic thing just your shtick to get clients, or to sidestep getting a private investigator's license?"

"Uh … well, it's fine if you don't believe that I'm psychic, but I believe that I'm psychic," he said, flustered. "And it might not have looked like I was using psychic power, I can understand that. I'm not even sure of that myself. But I suspect I was getting psychic inspiration on a subconscious level, which helped me figure things out."

"Interesting," she said.

"Indeed. I guess it doesn't matter how I do it, psychically or rationally, correct? The point is that I get results. And I was able to do that at St. Agatha's, so perhaps I'll be able to achieve the same thing with your daughter."

"Let's see how that unfolds." She smiled slightly.

He couldn't really even feel offended, because he was going to get paid regardless of what she believed. Shrinks are just plain bizarre, he thought.

"OK. So in rational real-world terms, what can you tell me about her?" He pulled his notepad and a pen out of his backpack and flipped to a blank sheet.

"Well, like I said before, she was difficult. We never really got along. She was a status climber, high-hatting me even when she was a teenager."

"I don't know what that expression means," Mason said, and wrote it down.

"High-hat? It means acting haughty to people you consider to be your social inferiors."

"I see."

"She'd date boys who would buy her things and then ditch them when the money dried up. We had some money, even when she was young. I'd say we were middle-class. But it was never good enough. That's the root of our discord."

"Was she involved in anything … uh … unsavory?" Mrs. Lewis hadn't implied anything like that, but he assumed Sherri's mother would be better informed.

"Do you mean illegal? Not that I know of. She didn't steal or do drugs; I would have known. It was about status for her, not about escaping reality or getting high."

"And how old is she now?"

"She'd be thirty-two. And again, to clarify, she's not missing. I guarantee that she's landed on her feet somewhere, but hasn't wanted to communicate with me or anyone at church because it's beneath her."

"I get the feeling that you're not really longing

for a reconciliation with her," he said, looking up from his note-taking.

"I have complex feelings. The bond we have with our children isn't just something you can switch off or forget about. But honestly, I just don't want to deal with her anymore at this point in my life. Not unless she's changed her attitude dramatically, and I don't anticipate that."

"Do you have a photo of her that I could take with me?" he asked.

She got up and lifted her handbag from behind her desk. She dug around in it and pulled out the snapshot she had taken from the church files on Friday. It was still folded in half.

"That's six or eight years ago now," Miss Cassie said.

"She looks so much like you." Mason put the photo and his notepad in his backpack. "And was there something metallic of hers that I could read? Humor me, here. It's my technique."

She pulled a small envelope from her handbag and handed it to him. He looked inside; it contained a thin silver chain with a tiny heart pendant, but he didn't take it out. So despite her stated disbelief in his psychic abilities, Mason realized, she had anticipated giving him this.

"She used to wear that all the time," she said.

"That's good. It should still have her energy. You remember how this works. I'll need silence for a few minutes."

"I'll be at my desk," she said, and walked over to it. It was far enough away that Mason felt secluded enough to focus, and her desk faced the windows rather than the sofa, so he felt comfortable, not being observed.

Sitting in the bright sunlight, he closed his eyes, cleared his head, and played Whac-A-Mole with the random thoughts that popped up, aiming to make his mind empty. A twinge of resentment about Miss Cassie not believing him popped up, but he pushed that down. And Ned, saying he could tolerate Mason's work but didn't think it was real, that was certainly irritating. How could he not trust me? he thought, and then pushed that away too. Eyes still closed, mind finally calm, he picked up the envelope and poured the necklace into his hand, covering it with his other hand and pressing them together. Almost immediately an image appeared: a simple diamond shape, like the symbol for the carpool lanes on the freeway, and the bus lanes downtown, but this one was dark green and three-dimensional. Each of its four segments had two or three facets, making it look like a complex crystal or a piece of jewelry.

"Wow," he said aloud and opened his eyes. He had never picked up such a strong image doing psychometry. Maybe it helped that he was annoyed with people, he thought. Maybe being in a slightly stressed head space was a psychic power enhancer.

"You've got something?" Miss Cassie said.

"Yes. This is exciting. Did Sherri have any other jewelry, maybe diamonds or something diamond-shaped?"

"Not that I recall."

"Huh." He frowned. "How about something green, like a green diamond, or maybe something set with emeralds?"

"No. She had some gold pieces, but nothing like that. I never gave her any of the family jewelry either."

"Well, whatever I was picking up, I'm sure it's important. It feels important."

She came back from her desk and sat opposite him, leaning forward. "So you're thinking that you're going to get somewhere with this."

"It feels like it, with such a strong image coming through."

"All right." She looked at him for a moment. "Now, Mason, however you proceed with this, remember that I don't want to talk to her. Don't tell her to call me, and don't tell her to visit me. You can tell her Betty hired you because she was worried."

"I can do that. Right now I need to figure out how I'm going to proceed. The necklace has given me a lead, believe it or not, but I need to figure out what it means."

"How long have you been using this psychic power of yours?" She leaned back in her chair.

"Well, I started in college. I did some course work on it, and I guess it's just always been something I did," he said.

"And how long have you been making your living at this?"

"It's actually fairly new. I worked for many years as a journalist, and I recently decided to make a career change. So far it's been going well, and the signs seem to indicate that I've made the right choice." It wasn't really a lie, he thought, brushing away a twinge of guilt at not telling her that he'd been doing it for less than a week, and that she was his first client.

"I know all about being self-employed. It can be scary, but it's also rewarding. So do you believe you have a unique and private connection to the other side, or whatever you call it?"

"I just call it reality, or maybe broader reality. 'The other side' implies a duality, over here and over there, like the living and the dead or something, but I don't think it's that simple. And yes, I have a unique connection. I think I'm able to tune in to things that other people ignore. Most people ignore it, but lots of people tune in. They might call it intuition, or for some people it's what they call creativity. But I think they're inspired by glimpses of a more realistic version of reality. What we usually perceive and focus on, I think, is just a tiny speck of the whole thing, the broader reality."

She nodded thoughtfully, not breaking eye contact. "You speak about it passionately."

"I guess I am passionate. It's probably a good thing, right, seeing as it's my career."

"And how do you structure your everyday reality? I mean things like the career change you mentioned, and even what to have for breakfast, or what you wear. Does it come from your own ideas, or do you look to friends and family for suggestions and advice?"

"Uh, I guess I'd have to say that I usually just

know." It was a weird question, he thought, almost like she was psychoanalyzing him. "Sometimes I'll take time to think about things, especially big decisions. I'll mull it over for a while, but eventually I always know what to do on my own. Although sometimes my boyfriend helps me decide what to wear. I have zero fashion sense—he's better with that stuff."

"You're gay. I hadn't picked up on that."

"Well, it's not like it matters for what we're doing." He smiled.

"So do you think this ability that you say you have, to tune in to extrasensory information that other people don't see, makes your life better, or does it get in the way of things you want to achieve?"

"It makes my life better, definitely. I'm trying to make a living from it, and I'm much happier doing this than when I was sitting in an office."

She glanced up at the wall clock. "I want to talk more about this," she said, "but I have a client coming soon, so I'm going to have to prepare for that."

"Of course," he said. "I'll get out of your hair." He picked up his backpack and headed for the door. "I'll be in touch when I know more."

"And vice versa. When you leave, could you slide the little sign on the outside of my door to the left so that it says 'Please knock'? Thanks."

What a weird woman, he thought as he rode down in the elevator. What a jumble of contradictions and confusion. He was trying to talk about finding her daughter, and she was on some crazy tangent about how he picked out his clothes.

RATHER THAN HEADING STRAIGHT home, he swung by the central library. It was a grand building befitting a major metropolis, part 1920s Egyptian temple complete with a crowning pyramid and part airy glass structure built in the 1980s. When he'd been single he used to come here sometimes just to browse and read; it was an energizing place that reminded him of how much potential there is in the world. He'd brought Ned here on one of their earliest dates, to look at the grand murals in the old part of the building; Ned had never seen them even though he'd grown up nearby. He had been so moved by the art, grand depictions of California history, that he got teary-eyed. He tried to hide it from Mason, but Mason had noticed, of course. Mason loved that he was so sensitive, and Ned loved that Mason could handle him expressing it; it turned out to be a perfect date. Mason still had no clue how some paint on a wall could move someone to tears, but it was like a space probe orbiting Saturn: he could at least marvel that such things were possible.

In any other building he would have walked down the steps to save time, but descending the multiple flights into the depths of the library, he took the escalator to enjoy the grandeur of the massive atrium, the neighboring office towers soaring overhead. He found a desk on a research floor and pulled out his laptop. Using the library's Wi-Fi, he started searching for green diamonds. The Web, naturally, brought up pages of gaudy jewelry for sale, an accounting business in Colorado Springs, more jewelry, a trash collection service in Australia, and a brand of tequila. He found a picture of the label, but the green diamond was solid and looked nothing like his psychic vision.

He started digging in the library's own catalog and databases, looking for green diamonds, green crystals, and even the carpool symbol. There were a few intriguing books that took him a few minutes to hunt down, but flipping through them brought no inspiration about Sherri. One news photo came up: it was a shoe store, photographed in the 1990s for its twentieth anniversary. The unremarkable owner, labeled by the photographer in the caption as "Ted Green, center, with glasses," had been caught by the camera in mid-guffaw, standing on the sidewalk in front of the business with a small crowd of people, probably shoppers and employees. The sign above the door, however, gave Mason a jolt of excitement. It had the shop's name, "Green's Diamond Shoe Mart," and beside it was a diamond-shaped logo—exactly the shape he had seen, complete with three-dimensional facets on each segment. He couldn't tell whether it was green because the photo was black-and-white, but this had to be it. Astonished, he stared at it for a few moments.

Maybe Sherri had worked there. Maybe the shop was still there. Green's was looking pretty tired in the nineties, but lots of beloved LA retail institutions were sagging and faded remnants of the twentieth century. The photo's caption said it was on Cahuenga in Hollywood; a good sign, he thought, because that part of the neighborhood hadn't yet been swept up in redevelopment. He pulled up a current street view, and sure enough, there it was, the same shabby sign above the same grungy doorway.

He had to go there; it was the simplest approach. Ted Green, by the looks of him in the news photo, would be dead or retired by now, but if it was still a family business, perhaps someone else would recognize Sherri. But it would have to wait until tomorrow—it was almost five o'clock, and Mason was supposed to buy tofu on the way home for tofu-and-tomatoes night.

"We should call you the tomato king," Peggy said. "You've grown some beauties this year." The three of them were sitting around the dining table that evening, the western sky still glowing orange. Ned had made a Caprese salad with marinated tofu in place of the mozzarella.

"Thanks, *chica,*" he said. "I think it's because it's been so hot, and tomatoes love the heat. So how's the boyfriend?"

"Van? On my nerves. I'm thinking it's time for a trade-in."

"Is he getting too serious?" he asked.

"No, he's just kind of a dud. I took him to the library, and his attention span imploded after about twenty minutes. It needs to be over. It's happening organically, though, because I think he feels the same way."

Mason nodded. Peggy changed boyfriends about

as regularly as he changed toothbrushes, which he did with fastidious regularity. "How was work?" he asked, to direct the conversation elsewhere.

"Ah, lawyers. You know how it goes." She waved her hand as if to brush the topic away. "I'm more interested in your day. So that woman from the church is a shrink?"

"Yes, and I realized today that she's a bit strange, which fits."

"How do you mean?" she asked.

"Well, you know, people who enjoy kids become teachers, people with psychological problems study psychology. And she does not have a healthy relationship with her daughter."

Ned chuckled. "Aren't you breaking some kind of client confidentiality by telling us about this?"

"I don't think so. Psychic practitioners aren't bound by any oath, at least not one that I've taken."

"Maybe you took it subconsciously, in the dream state," Ned said, deadpan.

Mason ignored him. "I think the people at the church know she doesn't get along with her daughter, because Mrs. Lewis knew all about it. So what I'm gossiping about is public knowledge, not privileged information. You could find it all out anyway if you were open-minded enough to use your own psychic power."

"Oh, of course, I should have thought of that," Ned said.

"So, what I want to know," Peggy said, "is what you're going to ask them at this shoe store, Mason. Will you lean on them, like in a detective novel?"

"I'm not going to lean on anyone," Mason said, his cheeks reddening at the thought. "I'm just going to show them her photo, and see if anyone recognizes her. But first I'm going to study up on how to read body language. That way I'll be able to tell if they're being truthful or not. I thought of that today. It's a great idea, right? Blending psychic and scientific methods."

"Can I see the photo?" Peggy asked.

They had finished eating, so Mason went to the office and got it from his backpack.

"She looks pretty ordinary," Peggy said. "Why did you fold it in half?" She passed the photo to Ned.

"Miss Cassie folded it, not me," he said. "I think the very image of her daughter was upsetting."

"Good-looking," Ned said, and handed it back.

"And I have something to show you," Peggy said, and padded down the hall to her room. She came back and laid a sheet of letter-size paper on the other end of the dining table. "I don't want to get food on it," she explained. Ned and Mason got up and moved around the table to look. She had done the artwork on her computer, and this was a printout. "It's solid black lines, with no gray, which makes it easier to reproduce," she said. "You can put it on cards in black-and-white, or add some color and put it on a website, or whatever."

Nearly filling the page, the main element of the logo was round, a crescent moon on the left side blending into a flaming sun on the right. The sun's rays that pointed directly to the right were slightly extended, making the overall image ovoid. In the middle of the sun-moon circle was the eye of Horus. Sometimes the ancient symbol was drawn with a full iris, and sometimes with a half iris that made it look drowsy. Peggy had used the half iris.

Mason examined it for a moment and said, "Peggy, this is absolutely brilliant. I love it. It's exactly right."

"Good, I'm glad," she said. "I'll send you the file so you can do what you want with it."

"Once I start making some dough," he said, "I'll pay you for it."

"Sure, that would be great."

"So, is the eye for extrasensory seeing?" Ned asked.

"It's the eye of Horus," Peggy said. "It just means protection. I was thinking that's what you're offering your clients, in a way. Protection, peace of mind, something like that. And it looks great, right?"

"I especially like the eye's sleepiness. It's exactly you," Ned said. "You could call yourself the afternoon psychic."

LATER, AS THEY WERE settling into bed, Mason asked Ned, "Did you really like the logo?"

"What matters is that you like it," he said, "and that it's appropriate for your business. I think it definitely fits, and I could see that you liked it."

"But is it good art?"

"That's a subjective question, but I'd say yes, it's art. The 'good' part is personal."

"I'll take that," Mason said. "I really do love it."

Mason wanted to try lucid dreaming again, to see if there was any way to get more information about Sherri, perhaps even to astrally project to where she was. Eventually he drifted into a dream with Peggy, rather than Sherri. Peggy was on stage, playing an electric guitar and smiling out at the audience. He was aware that he was dreaming, but he decided not to try to manipulate things, or to astrally project elsewhere, for fear of destabilizing things.

With his almost rational viewpoint, some of the surreal elements of the dream stood out. Peggy Pregnant would never pick up an electric guitar, he knew. More significantly, he had seen her gigs, and they were not bright and happy events where she smiled very much. Ned called her genre "depression music," but more charitably it might be labeled "dark folk music." Mason was in the audience watching her play, but the stage lighting was pointed at the spectators rather than at her. He could still see her, in that irrational way that dreams work, but the light was far too bright, glaring enough to hurt his eyes.

Mason knew that psychic insight can come from a whole panoply of sources: our own past or future selves, other parts of our overall self, even parallel realities where things work differently. He had no idea what he was seeing; perhaps an alternate Peggy who had gone electric, or a future version of her. It didn't seem to relate to Sherri in any way. Still, he had the sense that the information was valuable, something he'd asked for that was beyond a regular dream.

Later he found himself watching the logo that Peggy had drawn, but in the dream world it was in color: the moon part blue and the sun brilliant gold. The sun gradually brightened and overtook the moon side until the image was just the flaming sun. Just before he woke in the morning, he dreamed that the falcon-headed Horus was chasing him through the city, house to house, block to block. Sometimes Horus, who always appeared flat and two-dimensional, would get close enough that Mason could see the stylized teardrop below his drowsy eye, but Mason was afraid of him and kept running.

He struggled to find words to describe the imagery of the dreams when he woke up. "Peggy—happy—electric guitar—bright lights," he wrote. And instead of describing the Horus incident, he drew a sketch of the god running after him.

Tuesday

BY LUNCHTIME MASON HAD had breakfast and enough espresso to get to work. He sat on the balcony beside the tomato plants and pulled open his computer. He wanted to research how to interview people effectively to get information from them, and how to tell if they were lying or withholding something. There was a lot of dross on the topic, but eventually he found a couple of academic articles and a book that had the kind of information he wanted. Surprisingly, the best ideas for ferreting out details from reticent interviewees were directed at medical professionals, to establish a full picture of a patient's health.

Ned, who was working in the office, slid open the screen door and said, "Look at you, working at home."

"I'm loving this," he said.

"It's great to have you around. It feels like Saturday."

"Maybe we can have lunch in a while."

"I had lunch when you were finishing breakfast," he said, "but I appreciate the offer."

"I thought that was your midmorning snack."

"When the clock says high noon, it's called lunch."

"Weird logic, but if that's what makes you happy, who am I to argue. So what are you working on?" Mason asked.

"It's kind of interesting. This guy has refinanced his mortgage so many times, I can't figure out whether it's fraud or he's a financial genius." He leaned down to read Mason's computer screen. "'Conducting Effective Interviews with Reluctant Subjects, by Dr. Amos Friedman.' Who's that?"

"He's just some academic working for a health-insurance company. This is what your premiums are paying for. I think it'll help me figure out who's lying to me."

"Good luck with that. I hope old Amos knows what he's talking about."

An hour later Mason felt like he was ready to go to Green's Diamond Shoe Mart. First he made himself another pot of espresso and a little salad with cashews and almonds and cranberries. To create the atmosphere of authority he needed, he knew he had to wear the suit again. It didn't look that rumpled, he decided, despite Mrs. Lewis's dig, but he would get it pressed one of these days anyway. He opened Ned's side of the closet and picked out a dark necktie to go with it. That part of Hollywood was close enough to cycle to, but there was no way he was going to do that in a suit and dress shoes. He walked down the hill, pawing at his tie and readjusting it in a vain attempt to make it more comfortable, and took the metro; it was just a couple of stops.

He walked up out of the station into the shadow of massive high-rises crowded on land that had been a backwater zone of cheap tailors, wig stores, and vast surface parking lots just a few years before. With the arrival of the train, the area had been rezoned to encourage density, and it seemed to have worked—gleaming new condos and hotels were stacked almost on top of each other. A few blocks' walk led to a still ungentrified part of Hollywood, away from the boulevard, where small film-industry subcontractors, offices, and retail storefronts had languished mostly unaltered since the 1940s.

As he neared it, the shoe store looked even more run-down than its photos had implied. The interior was deserted when he walked in except for a middle-aged guy playing with a smart phone on the counter beside the cash register. There was a surprising amount of footwear—it seemed to be mostly women's boots, pumps, and sandals—on the racks, which were at least eight feet high and stretched far into the back of the store. The clerk glanced up with a look of utter boredom.

"We only sell women's shoes," he said, looking briefly down at Mason's oxfords and then back to his phone.

"Actually, I have something to show you," Mason said. He pulled off his backpack and found the photo of Sherri. "Do you know this woman?" he asked, handing it to him.

"Never seen her before. Is she missing or something?"

"Yes, she is. I've been told that she might have worked here, or maybe she was a customer here."

"She hasn't worked here recently. Not in my time, and I've been here for six years."

"Is there someone else who's been here for a while who might remember her as a customer?"

"Yeah, Carlos is friendly with lots of the ladies." He turned and shouted to the back of the store, "Carlos!"

Mason found it hard to believe this place had "lots" of customers, despite the extensive inventory. It almost felt like a fake, like a front for money laundering or something. But it was more likely that the business was just coasting through time with inertia, gradually becoming an anachronism.

Carlos was a thin Latino guy with a little mustache, probably in his thirties. He wore the same green suit jacket and tie as the other clerk, although Carlos's jacket looked pretty threadbare. "Can I help you?" he asked as he walked up to the counter.

"Do you know this woman?" Mason asked,

and slid the photo along the counter to him. Even before he spoke, Mason knew by his reaction that he was going to lie to him.

"I don't think so," he said, shrugging and glancing at the other guy. The shrug and the fact that his voice rose in pitch were classic signs of deception, according to Dr. Friedman. Carlos looked at Mason closely. "You a cop?"

He shook his head. "No, I'm not. But this is important. Listen, can we talk privately?" He looked pointedly at the other clerk.

"Not here," the other man said, and glowered at him.

"Well, then, Carlos, can I talk to you outside?" Mason said, and grabbed the photo of Sherri from the counter.

"Oh, man, c'mon," Carlos said, but he followed him out to the sidewalk. They stood facing each other out of sight of the other clerk, and Carlos folded his arms. "I don't need any trouble, stretch."

"I don't want to make any trouble, but I know that you know who she is. She's a little bit older now than in the picture, but I know you recognize her." He tried to be firm but not threatening, as Dr. Friedman had suggested.

"Do you know her?" Carlos asked.

"Never met her in my life."

"So why are you looking for her?"

"She's missing," Mason said, "and there are people who want to make sure she's OK."

"Jesus," he muttered. "Frickin' thieves."

"What?" Mason said, feeling a sudden surge of

fear. Thieves sounded like something to be afraid of. It didn't help that Carlos now looked worried. The image of a cornered rat came to mind.

"It's always the same with those guys." He rubbed his forehead absentmindedly. "OK, dude, listen. If I talk to you, you can't say it came from me, OK?"

Mason realized that Carlos thought he represented somebody else, somebody to be afraid of; maybe he thought he was one of the thieves. What the hell was this woman involved in?

"You have my word," Mason said.

Carlos made a "kff" sound and shook his head. "I heard that she was caught up with some powerful people. Underworld types. But I'm thinking you already know about that. If you don't already know her, I really don't think you want to go messing with her, regardless of who you work for. She never did anything to me, but I always had the feeling that she could be dangerous."

"In what way?" Mason asked, speaking calmly despite the tingling at the back of his neck.

"It was almost like she didn't care. That she'd do anything, you know, and it wouldn't bother her. She'd just step over you if you were in the way. So I just did whatever she said. It's like that expression, 'She talked a good game.' Whatever she said seemed like a good idea, even if it wasn't."

"How did you get to know her?"

"She used to come in here for shoes. I don't really know about the rest of it, the guys she was involved with; that was later. I just heard stories. I haven't seen her in a couple of years."

"You just sold her shoes? That's how you know her?"

"Well, she traded for shoes."

"What did she trade?"

"You know, we'd go on a date."

"What kind of date?"

"Oh, man," he said, and ran his fingers through his hair. "I'd take her in my car over behind the high school, where there's nobody walking by after dark."

"So you'd have sex?"

"Kind of. You know, just the express version." He mimed what looked like bouncing a basketball off his crotch.

"OK, so she'd blow you, and then you'd give her shoes?"

"Right. And that's all I had to do with her."

"Was she a full-time prostitute?"

He looked puzzled. "I don't think she was a prostitute. She just wanted shoes."

"Did she have a job? Do you know where she was living?"

"I don't know about any of that. You should know that."

"Don't tell me what I should know," Mason said forcefully. "I'm asking you some questions here." It was bluster for him to be so commanding, but he managed to sell it, and it seemed to work on Carlos.

"OK, OK," he said, holding his hands up, fingers spread. "All I know is that she worked at that strip club on Sunset by the freeway, the Toy Box. That's at least two years ago. I saw her there a couple of times. I don't go in there anymore."

"She was a stripper?"

"Yes. Her stage name was Champagne."

"What did you mean about thieves and underworld people?" Mason asked.

"That's not who's looking for her?" Carlos frowned.

"Was she involved with gangsters, or was she on drugs or something?"

"Hey, who are you, anyway?" he said slowly, his hands moving to his hips. He didn't look intimidated anymore. Mason saw that he was about to get angry.

"OK, Carlos," he said, "that just about wraps it up. You can forget you ever saw me." Mason turned and walked north on Cahuenga, back toward the boulevard and the metro, as quickly as he could without showing that he was afraid that he might get clobbered.

"Hey, man," Carlos shouted after him. "Who are you, anyway?"

Mason didn't respond and kept walking, but he glanced back after a few seconds. Carlos had broken into a jog, coming after him, the look on his face more quizzical than angry.

"Yo, albino man! You said you were one of them. Come back here," he shouted.

Mason glanced back again, and seeing that Carlos was getting much closer, broke into a run. Even in a suit he knew that he should be able to keep ahead of the guy. One great side effect of cycling was that he had strong legs, and his height gave him a speed advantage. He flew around the corner onto Hollywood Boulevard, suit jacket billowing behind him, pedestrians on the busy sidewalk gaping at the flustered redhead. He managed another glance behind him, and saw that Carlos had stopped at the corner, watching him run. The guy probably didn't want to abandon his job for too long.

Mason was stunned—partly at being chased up the street, partly at Sherri's bizarre story, and mostly that the psychic lead had panned out. It was exhilarating to escape in one piece, he thought, ducking into the metro station and trotting down the stairs. He was also proud of himself for the veneer of authority he'd maintained with the guy. It could have backfired, but it had worked. Mason thought he had probably learned more than he would have if he'd approached Carlos in a friendly way, which would have been his instinct before he'd read up on interviewing.

On the train home he did some slow breathing to calm down. He'd never taken a yoga class, but it had become ubiquitous in LA after Madonna had promoted it, and he had learned some of the breathing techniques by osmosis. He pulled his yellow notepad out of his backpack and wrote down everything he'd learned from Carlos, then reread it.

   - Carlos, clerk at Green's Diamond Shoe Mart
   - traded Sherri blow jobs for shoes

   - worked at Toy Box: strip club on Sunset
    (2+ years ago)
   - stage name Champagne
   - "thieves"?

What am I getting into? he wondered. Carlos clearly assumed he was someone to be afraid of, someone involved with criminals, which implied that Sherri must be mixed up with criminals. Or at least she had been in the past.

Now Mason knew where to look next.

PEGGY GOT HOME FROM work just after Mason had changed out of his suit. Ned was on a work call in the office, so it didn't seem like he'd be cooking anytime soon. Mason went into the kitchen to assess what food they had available, pulling open cupboards and sticking his head into the refrigerator.

"Any dinner ideas?" he asked as Peggy walked in the kitchen.

"There should be lots of veggies in there. Stir-fry?"

"Sounds good. I have some news about the mysterious Sherri."

"I have news too. Let me change, and we'll talk." Her hair was piled on her head in great loops, but wisps of it were starting to escape.

Mason pulled out the veggies that he guessed might be compatible with a stir-fry, and soon his roommates came in.

"You stir, I'll chop," Peggy said to Ned, who put on an apron. She set to work cutting vegetables, and Ned pulled out the wok and put it on the stove. Mason got out of the way and sat facing them from across the counter.

"How did it go at the shoe store?" Ned asked.

"Kind of great," Mason said. "One of the clerks knew Sherri."

"Really?" Ned looked skeptical. "So you actually got a valid lead from touching the woman's necklace?"

"You really are psychic," Peggy said, staring at him in astonishment.

"Not that you ever doubted it," Mason said.

"So was Sherri a customer at the shoe store?" Peggy asked, ignoring Ned's scowl.

"In a way," Mason said. "She used to trade this clerk blow jobs for shoes."

"You can do that?" she said, incredulous. "I wish I'd known that. I would have a lot more shoes right now."

"That's kind of sleazy," Ned said. "Why would this guy admit that to you?"

"He thought I was working for someone else, maybe a gangster or somebody that she was mixed up with. I guess I 'leaned on him,' to use Peggy's phrase."

"Mason, that's terrifying," he said. "Do you really think it's safe to be lying to people that might do you harm?"

"I didn't pose as someone that I'm not. He kind of assumed I was dangerous, and I just didn't correct him. So it's not really scary, it's just effective interview tactics."

"But, I mean, you're putting yourself in danger.

Do you really want to be mixed up with that kind of thing?"

"No, but I'm already in it." He decided not to tell them about getting chased up the street.

"Ned," Peggy said, her hands full of sliced bok choy, "move it." He stepped out of her way, and she dropped the bok choy into the wok, which hissed and popped. Peggy took over stirring.

"But it's not some kid stealing from a church anymore," Ned said. "It's criminals and prostitutes. People who tend to be involved with firearms, which you don't do, remember?"

"She wasn't a prostitute; she just wanted shoes."

"It's just like Tintin," Ned said, folding his arms across his chest. "You said it last week. He always said 'I don't use guns,' but then there must be a dozen times where he's walking around with a pistol or a rifle and shooting at people. And worse, they're shooting at him."

"I'm not going to get into that kind of trouble. I know how to look out for myself."

"Did he know where to find her?" Peggy asked.

"He said he hadn't seen her for a couple of years, but at the time she was working as a stripper," Mason said. "Her stage name was Champagne. So that's the next thing: I'm going to the Toy Box on Sunset, the gentlemen's club where she worked."

Ned stared at him, mouth agape.

"They've co-opted that word," Peggy said, looking up from the wok. "You're not going to find guys in spats and top hats and tails like in a 1930s movie. They're just guys leering at naked women.

Nothing gentle about them."

"I'm not too worried about the guys," Mason said. "I'm hoping she'll still be working there."

"And then you'll take this news back to her mother?" Ned said. "Blow jobs for shoes, and working in strip clubs?"

"The truth isn't always pretty. Honestly, though, I have no idea yet what I'm going to tell her mother."

"Grab your plates, boys, this is ready," Peggy said. They filled their plates from the wok and sat at the dining table.

"I just don't know if there's any point in pursuing this if she's in a situation that you wouldn't want to tell her mother about," Ned said. "Their relationship is broken, and I don't know how you'd use that information to fix it."

"It's not so much their relationship," Mason said. "I'm not going to get in the middle of that. Her mother doesn't even know if she's alive."

"Maybe you can just tell Miss Cassie that her daughter's fine, and let that be the end of it," he said.

"But I don't know yet if she's fine," Mason said, exasperated. "This information is two years old."

"I don't think you can quit now," Peggy said. "At least find her and talk to her. That way, you'll have earned your fee. You can gloss over the rough parts with her mother, but at least get all the details together first."

Ned sighed. "Well, if you're going to this gentlemen's club, I'm going too. There's no way I'm going to let you walk into a place like that alone."

"Oh, Edgar," Peggy said. "*You* are a *real* gentleman."

"You'd come with me even though you think I'm delusional?"

"I never said you were delusional," he said, reaching over and squeezing Mason's hand. "Besides, I wouldn't miss seeing you in a strip club."

"Well, I would feel safer with you there," Mason said. "Can we go tomorrow?"

Ned chuckled. "We're going on a date to a strip club."

"Peggy, you said you had news?" Mason said.

"Indeed. I called an old friend of my mom's today, Helen, and we talked for over an hour."

"Did she know anything about your father?"

"Not really. We mostly talked about my mother. She had a lot of great stories from back in the day, but not about guys my mom was involved with. Helen said she kept that part of her life private. I guess people did back then. She and my mom worked together at a place called the Lounge in Koreatown, but it was a few years before I was born."

"That would have been before it was even called Koreatown," Ned said.

"When I was at the library I found out that she lived over there back then, so it fits."

"What did they do at this lounge?" Mason asked.

"They were waitresses, and it was an upscale place, a good job. Helen said they had to hustle, but they got tipped well. She said there was a dress code, and they had to wear short skirts and panty hose."

"Ouch," Mason said.

"Can you imagine? It must have been suffocating," she said. "I don't think I've ever worn pantyhose."

Mason shook his head. "It wouldn't be a good look with your faux pregnancy."

"I know I've never worn them," Ned said.

"I think there may be photographic evidence to invalidate that statement," Mason said.

"What, you mean at Halloween in Boys Town? That doesn't count."

"You wore panty hose for Halloween?" Peggy asked.

"Technically they were tights, and it was part of my costume."

"Potayto, potahto," Mason said.

"Come on, I was Peter Pan. I had no choice."

"I'm sorry I missed that," she said.

"Did Helen have any ideas about who else might have known your dad?" Mason asked.

"Not really, but I know some other friends of my mom's who would have known her in the early eighties."

"I thought of another possibility," Mason said.

"What's that?" she asked.

"Well," he hesitated, "it's somewhat delicate."

"Jesus, Mason, we're not Victorians. Out with it," she said.

"I wondered if maybe the reason your mom kept your father's identity secret from you was that he was a relative. Or something like that."

"You know, I actually thought of that myself at one point. So it's not a shocking new idea, and you certainly don't have to be afraid to talk about it. When we studied genetics in junior high science—I must have been, what, about thirteen—I went home and asked her flat-out if that was her secret."

"And what did she say?"

"She laughed, and she promised it was nothing like that. She said that my grandfather had been a respectable guy, and there weren't any other male relatives around. My father was a decent guy too, she said, but there was to be no more talk of him. I believed her, I think, because she had been in her twenties, living on her own, and working by the time she got preggers. And the way she characterized him as a decent guy made me think that it wasn't a sexual assault or something. So I've always had the idea that he was just a boyfriend, and I was an accident."

"Are you going to talk to her other friends?" Mason said.

"That's my next step," she said. "There's still hope."

"All right," Ned said, and got up from the table. "Thanks for cooking, Peggy, it was lovely."

"I'll clean up," Mason said.

"Thanks, babe. I'm going to excuse myself and go do some reading."

When Ned had gone, Peggy said, "You should be very proud of yourself for having that kind of psychic breakthrough. You were just sitting in that woman's office?"

"Just sitting there on her sofa in the sunshine. I was actually a bit miffed, because she doesn't believe I used any kind of paranormal skill to figure out the thing at St. Agatha's. And then bam, this powerful image came to me. I wondered if being in that frame of mind enhanced my psychic abilities."

"Poor Mason. Nobody seems to believe you."

"And yet I'm getting results and making serious headway. And I'm the crazy one."

"It doesn't really matter what other people think," she said. "You must know that by now."

"I know it doesn't matter that much, but it does matter when it's my boyfriend," Mason said. "It's almost like there's a fundamental distrust there."

"I think he's just got that kind of mind. It's like the religious people that piss him off so much; he has the same kind of dogma, but from a scientific perspective. And it doesn't mean that he doesn't trust you. He needs time to come to accept what you're doing."

"That's optimistic, at least," he said.

"Well, I think it's true. You have to admit it's a pretty big leap for him."

"You don't seem to have any doubts about my new career path."

"All I can do is take it at face value," Peggy said. "Whether I understand the mechanism or not, I can see you're accomplishing something."

"Sexy time?" Mason asked Ned when they climbed into bed that night.

"How could I resist such an eloquent overture?"

he said. Mason straddled him and playfully grabbed his hands.

"I think this leaning on people makes you feel virile," Ned said.

"So maybe I should mess you up a little."

"Bring it on," Ned said, and pulled him down to kiss him.

Afterward Mason gave himself the autosuggestion to acquire dream-world insights into Sherri and her motivations. Eventually he found himself on a white-sand beach with palm trees, walking along, feeling the sand crunch under his bare feet. He knew he was dreaming, but was able to ignore that realization effectively enough not to destabilize the dream. The cozy stretch of beach and turquoise water—it was Saint Martin, he realized, the soft Caribbean color palette nothing like California's cold, majestic seascapes. He and Ned had gone to the Dutch part of the island the winter before to try scuba diving.

There was someone behind him, he realized, and he whirled around. It was a chubby guy in a three-piece suit, smiling gently at him. He felt it again, someone behind him, and turned around again to confront the same guy, or maybe it was someone else just dressed the same. That's an Englishman's suit, Mason thought, with pinstripes almost too broad to be taken seriously, the fabric a shade too blue. The suited men didn't say anything but remained on either side of him. When he turned his head again he realized they were now four, just beyond the reach of his arms, one in each direction, so that he couldn't see them all at once. He didn't feel crowded or afraid; they shuffled in the sand mirthfully, almost dancing, waving their arms. They didn't seem insistent, but he felt that perhaps they were trying to show him something. Around they went, the four of them, and Mason had to laugh at their silly dance and animated expressions.

He wanted to determine whether they were the same person or four different guys, but as he tried to focus on them, to manipulate the dream, it slipped away. When he woke up, he remembered it in detail. He knew it was probably important because it had been so vivid, but he had no idea what it meant. He wrote down the key points on his bedside notepad, and added a little sketch of the configuration: the four suits with him at the center.

Wednesday

ONCE HE WAS AWAKE and sufficiently caffeinated, Mason went into the office and found the notes he'd made about St. Agatha's. They filled about a dozen sheets of a yellow notepad. He tore off the pages and put them in a legal-size file folder. On the tab he wrote "St. Agatha's." After thinking about it for a moment, he added "Solved." He tucked it in the front of his drawer in the file cabinet. He tore his notes about Sherri from the notepad and put them in their own folder. This one he labeled "Sherri Millar."

He reread the notes he'd made to try to get a clearer image of who this person was. Basing

anything on what her mother had said was difficult, because it was completely one-sided. There
are always two sides to a disagreement, and Sherri
might have her own horror stories about Miss Cassie. From what he'd been told, Sherri was a manip-
ulative social climber who valued status above
everything else. If that was the case, it didn't make
sense that she was involved with gangsters or working as a stripper. Both things might be a means to
an end, but not after several years; an ambitious
person would have moved on by then. The Toy Box
seemed like a long shot; it was unlikely that she'd
still be working there, unless she had fallen into
drug use. Even ambitious junkies tend to get stuck
in one place.

Mason thought that going to a strip club with
Ned was like a pair of dolphins visiting Albuquer-
que: it was far from their daily reality, and what to
expect was beyond them. They were in their bedroom on Wednesday afternoon after Ned had finished work, and Mason was trying to get dressed.

"What do straight guys wear?" he said, frus-
trated, digging through his closet. "Or should I
say, what do gentlemen wear? I've never been to
a gentlemen's club. What kind of look should I be
working?"

"Nobody's going to be looking at you," Ned
said, "so it doesn't really matter what you're working. Go with jeans and a dress shirt."

"Have you ever been to one of these places?"

"Of course. My brothers took me when I was a

teenager. It was like a rite of passage."

"How could you get into a bar as a teenager?"

"Not all of them serve booze. I think the Toy Box does, but others are eighteen-and-over."

"How do you know this stuff?" he said, amazed.

Ned put on black jeans and a royal-blue dress shirt unbuttoned to the middle of his chest. He looked sexy, but still, he wouldn't have been out of place in a business meeting, Mason thought. Somehow Ned always managed to look more polished than he ever could; he looked more dressed up now than Mason would have in his suit. Mason's pant legs would gradually ride up to expose his drooping socks and shocking white legs while Ned's broke perfectly all evening in any position he took. Mason couldn't keep a shirt tucked in for more than twenty minutes, while Ned's always looked like he'd been ironed into it. Going out with him probably made Mason look even more disheveled in contrast, but he didn't really mind. It was mystifying more than it was frustrating, and he found it entertaining to be out with someone that people enjoyed looking at. It was such an ego boost: this guy was widely desirable, and he had chosen to be with Mason.

"Should we take the Barracuda?" Ned asked as they left the house.

"I don't know if we need to draw any more attention to ourselves than necessary."

"The Crown Vic it is, then."

It was a huge car, by modern standards, but Ned skillfully managed the narrow and winding hillside streets out of their neighborhood, down to the boulevard. Mason clicked on the radio and fiddled with the tuning knob until he found a station with music that he liked.

"House music," Ned commented.

"Indeed. It has a good beat, and you can dance to it. Ergo, it's good music. I can write that down for you on a little index card if you'd like, to help you remember. And I present that not as an opinion or a belief, but as objective knowledge gathered from four hundred years of scientific developments."

"Are you sure you don't want to find some burlesque tunes to put you in the mood for our date?"

"Is there even a station that plays that? It seems unlikely. A lot of them play that polka music your dad always has on."

Ned laughed. "It's not polka music. It's called mariachi, and it's a storied and respectable genre."

"It has a polka beat, and you can polka to it. You don't like it either; I know you don't."

"Damn, Mason, you're so Anglo sometimes."

Mason was about to respond, but Ned said, "Look, we're here. There's the sign for the Toy Box. I don't suppose you want me to park in their lot."

"No. Something tells me to keep some distance."

Ned turned at the next corner and deftly swung into an open space on the side street. They walked back to the front door of the Toy Box, Mason's heart pounding, and got past the burly bouncer, who checked their IDs. It was about 5:30, and the place had just a few customers. The main room seemed dark after coming in from broad daylight. A lone dancer gyrated around one of the poles on the stage, Mason saw when his eyes had adjusted. She looked bored and wasn't even fully undressed. He stopped near the entryway and gaped for a moment at her exaggerated voluptuous curves, but Ned poked him and took him to a table far from the active pole but with a good view of the room. A couple of the other patrons glanced up at them as they walked in, but they seemed mostly disinterested in them, the dancer, or anything else.

When they sat down, Ned grabbed his arm, and in a low voice said, "I don't want to alarm you, but there's an almost completely naked woman up there by that fire pole on the stage."

"Quit it," Mason said. "This is already unnerving enough. You can swagger in here like you own the place, but I feel like I'm on another planet."

Ned laughed. "Have you even seen a naked woman before?"

"Of course. Sheesh, I'm not a square. I'm sure I must have seen one in a biology textbook at some point."

A waitress in a low-cut, tight black dress came over and put two napkins on the table. Ned ordered tonic water, and Mason ordered beer. When she brought them, Mason handed her a twenty and asked, "Is Champagne working tonight?"

"She'll be in around six." Her eyes narrowed. "I haven't seen you in here before."

"Yeah, well, I haven't been in a while."

"He wants to arrange a private dance with her," Ned said.

"I'll let her know," the waitress said, winking at him and setting the change on their table.

"Why did you do that?" Mason asked him when she had left. "I don't want a private anything."

"It's the only way you'll get a chance to talk to her. You can't just start in on her about her mother or whatever if she's up there working a pole."

"The last thing I need is a naked woman getting up in my grill."

"Well, it's your job now," Ned said, and giggled.

Mason found it mildly annoying that Ned was so amused at his discomfort. "You don't feel sorry for me at all," he said.

"Of course not. This is hilarious."

Mason switched from beer to tonic water for their second round. On the stage a series of dancers came and went; some undressed more than others, but none of them got completely naked. The dancing was perfunctory, and even the clients who watched intently seemed bored. Mason didn't think he was really a prude, but the jiggling and gyrating seemed more gritty than erotic to him.

"Why is there a black light above the pole?" he asked Ned.

"It must hide the blotchy skin or cellulite or something. They've all been pretty curvy."

"They are good-looking. But the pole thing is kind of inelegant."

Ned snorted. "I don't think anyone comes here looking for elegant. What I want to know is, how come they're not taking it all off? I wonder if it's something to do with the liquor license."

"Just be grateful that's all there is to see," Mason said.

Sometime after six, he noticed a scantily clad woman over by the bar, with a wide, surreal platinum-blond afro, talking to their waitress. She wore a gold lamé halter top tied with a big knot in front under her ample bosoms, along with matching hot pants.

"It's not every day you see gold lamé hot pants," he said.

"If you were the kind of guy who came in here regularly, you'd see them all the time. And they're called booty shorts these days."

"Really?" Mason said. "Why do they need a new name? They look exactly the same as they do in sixties movies."

"Heads up," Ned said, and nodded toward the bar. The blond was walking over to their table with a wide grin on her face.

"Which one of you wants a dance with Champagne?" she asked.

"It's for him," Ned said, slapping Mason on the back.

"Well, then, come with me, darlin'," she said.

Mason stood to follow her and looked for encouragement from Ned, but he was laughing.

The blond led him down a hallway into one of several tiny, dark back rooms. There was a chair against the back wall, facing a stool in the middle of the room.

"Have a seat," she said, pointing to the chair. "It's fifty for fifteen minutes. I can touch you, but you can't touch me."

An hour of this, he thought, would burn up his entire fee from the church job. He sat down and said, "So where's Champagne?"

"You're looking at her, baby." She fluffed her massive hair with one hand and frowned. "Didn't you ask for me?"

"I did, but I was expecting someone else. She's a little older than you, worked here about two years ago and used the same name, Champagne."

"Darlin', I'm the one and only Champagne." She smiled seductively and knelt on the stool, alarmingly close to his knees.

"Wait, wait. Look at this." Mason pulled Sherri's photo from his shirt pocket and held it out to her. "It's a picture of the old Champagne. Do you know her?"

Her face hardened, and he knew that she recognized her. "Never seen her before. And she's not here; you get me instead. Younger skill set." She gestured to her ample breasts.

"Nothing personal, but I'm not interested in you. I need to talk to this woman. I know you know who she is."

She stared at him for a moment, as if deciding what to do. "Get out," she said, standing up and folding her arms.

"You know her," Mason said. "Where can I find her?"

"Are you a cop?"

"No, I'm not. But I can get the cops involved easily enough. You'll have to think about whether you really want that or not. I just need to talk to her." He waved the photo and thought about standing up too, but decided it might be more effective to appear unfazed.

"No way. I don't know anything about any of it. I hardly knew her. And she's long gone."

"You're lying," he said calmly. "And if I was your boss, I'd be pretty upset at someone dragging the police into my place of business."

"Who the hell are you?" she asked.

"A concerned citizen."

He couldn't tell if she was afraid of him, but she was clearly worried by the suggestion of calling the police. She glared at him for a few seconds, calculating. But then her face softened; she had made her decision. "OK. Maybe I do know her. She helped me get started here. My grandmother in the business, so to speak. But when she retired, she made it very clear that she wanted to make a clean break from this life."

"OK," he nodded, breathing deeply to keep himself calm, and waited for her to continue.

"She was involved with some rough people. I know enough about it that I know you're not one of them." She reached up to her neck, not taking her eyes off him, and fondled the pendant on her necklace, sliding it back and forth on its chain. "But I also know she wouldn't want you to escalate your inquiries."

"And neither would you, I suspect."

"True." She grinned. "Give me your phone number, and give me a couple of days. I'll see if I can find her. She might be on the other side of the world right now, I honestly don't know."

"OK," he said, standing up. "It's a deal. And if I don't hear from you, I'll be back over the weekend."

Weird, he thought, she had her phone concealed in her skimpy top. She pulled it out and punched in his number as he recited it. He ducked out through the curtain, and she yelled after him, "Hey, ginger snap! You owe me fifty bucks."

He turned back and pulled his wad of cash out of his pants pocket, peeling off two twenties and then digging in his pocket again for a couple of fives. When he handed it over, it quickly disappeared into her clothing.

"You know, whoever you are, you really don't want to mess with her," she said.

"And you don't want to mess with me," he said, smiling. He was sure that he came across as confident, but it was just bravado; her words had made his heart pound. With any luck the poor lighting would mask the red that had inevitably risen in his cheeks.

Back in the main room, he motioned to Ned that it was time to go. Ned took a quick last swig of his tonic water and stood up to meet him at the door. "Check and see if we're followed," Mason said quietly.

Ned looked back a couple of times on the walk to the car. "Nobody's following us. The bouncer didn't even watch us leave. So who was the phony blond? Did you find Sherri?"

It hadn't actually crossed his mind that the blond afro was fake, but it made sense. Ned was so much more observant about those kinds of things. Mason never noticed who had breast implants and who didn't, or who had had cosmetic surgery, but Ned always knew.

Mason told him the gist of his meeting with Champagne. When they reached the car, he said, "Do you want to eat somewhere?"

"Sure, if you'll text Peggy and tell her we won't be home. How about the Indian place?"

"Perfect," Mason said.

Ned negotiated the Crown Vic back onto the boulevard. "It sounds like you did the leaning-on-people thing again. You're not concerned about the element of danger?"

"It's terrifying," Mason said. "But I don't really plan on calling the police. I don't know about anything illegal, although all these people have implied that there's something shady with Sherri. Her own mother called her a chiseler. I mentioned the cops as a bluff to see if this woman would react. She did, which means she has reasons of her own to be afraid of them."

"Or maybe a reason to be afraid of Sherri."

"Let's hope not," he said, but he realized that Ned had a point. The shoe-store guy had said she was dangerous. "Anyway, I'm not planning on meeting anyone at an abandoned warehouse at two a.m. or anything. I think I'll be safe enough if I use common sense."

"Says the man who puts more faith in his psychic sense."

"I have common sense too, in equal proportion to my psychic powers."

"You say that," he said, glancing over at Mason and giving him a quick once-over, "but then I look at that shirt you're wearing, and seriously, man, I have to question whether you have any sense at all."

Mason laughed. "If I'm not mistaken, you bought me this shirt."

"In the store it didn't make the mannequin look like a homeless Quaker."

"Oh!"

"You know I'm kidding, right?"

"And yet the kernel of truth is still there. I guess I could run the iron over it when it goes through the laundry. Do we even have an iron?"

"Do you even know how laundry works?"

"It's that big white box with the porthole in it, out in the garage, right? I would totally do it if I felt safe about it. My issue is that when there's a pile of rags out there, I can never be sure whether it's trash, or cleaning rags, or part of your summer wardrobe."

"Your issues run a lot deeper than that, my sweet," Ned said, taking his hand and kissing the back of it.

THE INDIAN RESTAURANT WAS a family-run place, and the owner cheerfully pointed out the dishes that were made vegan.

"So you really don't mind walking into a bar and

sitting with me while I drink a beer?" Mason asked.

"Not at all. It's not a trigger for me."

"What's a trigger?"

"Something that reminds you of getting drunk and might trigger you to relapse."

"So what are your triggers?"

"Well … airplanes," Ned said. "They used to give you free booze when you flew overseas. So I'd drink for four hours until I was hammered, sleep for six hours, and wake up in Tokyo. I still get a little twinge now and then when I'm on an airplane."

"Interesting. What else?"

"Sometimes when you and Peggy drink red wine with dinner. I feel a bit left out of the fun."

"You know, she probably figured that out, because recently she always says no to wine with dinner. I guess I should have realized that too. I'm sorry I'm not very tuned in."

It's not your responsibility," Ned said. "If I couldn't handle it, I would have said something. Even though I feel it, I don't think it's going to make me relapse."

"You know, she's really intuitive. We're kind of lucky to have her around."

"She's wise beyond her years."

WHEN THEY GOT HOME Peggy was sitting at the dining table with several photo albums stacked around her. They were coil-bound and had covers with colorful scenes of flowery landscapes and sailboats, unmistakably 1980s. Mason assumed they were her mother's.

"So how are my gentlemen this evening?" she asked.

"I got Mason a lap dance," Ned said. He started to unbutton his shirt and headed down the hall to change his clothes.

"Ha!" she cackled. "I wish I'd been able to see that."

"It didn't get very far," Mason said, and sat with her at the table.

"Aren't you going to shower?"

"Uh … no. It's not like I had sex with anyone. We just went in and drank, like in a bar."

"But you had a lap dance."

"Not really," he said. "I derailed the dancing part so that I could talk to her."

"But you sat down."

"Well, yeah."

"In the lap-dance chair."

"Yes."

"OK, just think about that for a minute before you decide whether you're going to shower or not," she said.

"Thanks for that, Peggy. Maybe I'll just burn my clothes instead."

"So the lap dancer, was it her?"

"Her name was Champagne, but it wasn't Sherri. She's using the same stripper name that Sherri was using a few years ago."

"Is there a connection between them? Maybe Sherri is her stripper mother or something."

"She actually said that, although I think she said 'grandmother.' She wasn't really forthcoming at first, but I talked her into connecting me with Sherri. I guess I leaned on her, in a way."

"So did you get her phone number or something?"

"She's going to have Sherri call me, she said. And I threatened to come back and bother her if she didn't do it."

"That's pretty exciting," Peggy said. "It sounds like you're getting close."

"I hope so. What's with the photo albums?" Mason asked.

"Just digging into my mother's life a little more. After I talked to her friend Helen, I thought of looking for other people in all the photos from back then. Maybe I can show some of them to Helen and it'll remind her of these people and maybe their names. Look at this one." She flipped to a page in the top album. Nothing was labeled. Among the photos stuck to the yellowing board beneath the page's plastic cover sheet was one of a pair of young women standing in front of a set of heavy wooden doors. A poster for a band, Cuba Libre, was mounted next to the door, and white lettering on the awning above read "Helios." They were posing for the camera and smiling.

"Is that your mom?"

"Yes, on the left. I have no idea who her friend is. Maybe Helen will know her."

"It's definitely the late seventies, or very early eighties," he said. Both women wore what looked like shimmering polyester, in vibrant saturated colors. Peggy's mom wore a powder-blue pant suit over a blouse in a red-and-white bubble pattern, and her friend wore a lime-green halter top and high-waisted flared white trousers.

"Definitely. I looked up this name, Helios, and it was a nightclub in Koreatown back then. It was upscale, like the one she worked at, and it had live music. I think she might have worked there. Isn't that kind of the vibe in the photo, like they're on the way to work?"

"They're not dressed to go to a club, and it's daytime, so yeah, maybe. But maybe they were sightseeing?"

"She lived here, so I don't think she would have been excited about taking a photo of the door to a nightclub in broad daylight. I think it was their first day of work, or maybe they just got hired on, so they posed with the awning. Couldn't those be job-interview outfits?"

"Could be," Mason said.

Peggy tapped the photo with her finger. "I'd love to talk to this woman, whoever she is. I'll talk to Helen again, show her this and find out if she knows her. Maybe she'll remember something about this place, like whether my mother worked there. I know she worked at a few different clubs, and even downtown at the Biltmore for a while. She had a thing for musicians and that whole world."

"You know what else you could do," he said. "You can figure out what year it is. Look at the poster beside them. It's for a performance at this club, right, because it says Helios right at the bottom, so it has to be current with when the photo was taken.

Check out the date. There's no year written, but—"

"You're right! Saturday, May 21. That has to correspond to a specific year. May 21 would be on a different day each year." She leapt up and hurried down the hall, returning moments later with her computer in hand. A few keystrokes later, she found it. "It was 1983," she said. "The year before I was born."

"So that's another piece of data that might tweak Helen's memory."

"That was brilliant, thank you," she said.

"Is he reading your jewelry?" Ned said as he came into the room, looking more relaxed now in a T-shirt, and sat down with them.

"Peggy was just telling me that her mom liked the music clubs back in the day. Look at her here," Mason said, and twisted the photo album toward him. "That was in 1983."

"Great outfit," he said. "So did she date music people too?"

"If she was working in live-music places," Mason said, "it makes sense that she'd be around lots of musicians."

"I remember her dating a couple of guys like that in the nineties. There was one who was a drummer. He was the strangest guy. They say that about drummers, 'beware.' She never really got too serious with any guys that I remember. Eventually I think she quit trying."

"Do you think you got interested in music because of your mom's connection to that world?" Mason asked.

"I never really thought about it, but you know, I learned to play on a guitar that had been left at our house. So maybe indirectly her musician friends got me involved."

"What about Peggy Pregnant?" Mason said. "Do you think there's any connection between that persona and not knowing your dad?"

"I guess there might be a connection. The image of the pregnant performer was just happenstance. I found the belly thing, and it made me laugh. It fit so well with the music I was playing then: old Joni Mitchell, Joan Baez, Carole King, and some of my own stuff. The image resonated with the music, and audiences were into it.

"But maybe on some deeper level I was fascinated with pregnancy because my mother had obscured that part of her life, my life, from me. I thought she would tell me about it one day."

"At least you've got some good leads," Mason said.

"I wish I had your psychic powers," she said, and smiled.

ALL THE GYRATING EXPOSED flesh at the Toy Box must have had an effect on Ned, Mason realized, because when they climbed into bed that night, Ned was insistently amorous. After they'd had sex, it took a while for Mason to fall asleep.

Who were the guys on the beach? he wondered, remembering his vivid dream of the night before. He mentally threw the question out in all directions. Why were they significant?

In the dream state they found him again, the four blue-suited men. They were on a narrow country road, and the four of them flanked Mason on either side, leading him up a hill. He walked with them, and they looked straight ahead and wouldn't meet his eye. They walked briskly, but he had no trouble keeping up. He was aware he was dreaming, which was a victory of sorts, but again he decided not to try to manipulate the dream. It seemed like he was supposed to follow again, not lead.

The suits seemed intent on reaching a structure at the top of the hill, a squat building made of fieldstone. As they got closer he saw a wooden cross—a church. Could this be about St. Agatha's? They came up on the fieldstone fence that ran around the building, and suddenly, in that way that dreams unfold, they were inside the building. The four of them faced one another, as they had on the beach, but this time Mason wasn't among them— he stood outside the circle. They weren't focused on him at all, but spoke in low voices, too low for him to understand. Mason tried to look at the building itself, but before he could get a bead on it, they were all outside again, near the fieldstone fence. But now the fence ran into the distance in both directions, straight and unbroken but undulating over the hills. The suits stood on the other side of it now, where the hill dropped sharply downward. It was getting dark, and they set off walking down the hill. He felt that he wasn't supposed to follow them; it was an unspoken prohibition that he just knew. They were going, and he couldn't follow them. One of the four looked back across the fence at him, just for a moment, and met his eye, but then they were lost in the gloom.

He willed himself to wake up, and then clicked on his bedside light and pulled his notepad and pen out of the nightstand drawer. He scrawled down as much about the dream as he could, in loopy drifting script because his eyes were still half closed.

Thursday

NED GENTLY SHOOK MASON awake in the morning. He was already up and dressed for a home-office workday. "What's your schedule like today?" he asked.

Mason groaned, irritated at being awakened against his will. "I was going downtown to do some research in the library this afternoon. What time is it now, like six? Why are you up so early?"

"It's more like ten. Gilbert's coming over this morning if you want to have coffee with us. If not, go back to sleep."

"Yeah, OK," he said, and rolled onto his back, blinking to force his eyes to stay open. Mason had mixed feelings about Gilbert. He was one of Ned's close friends from childhood, and he had to respect that, but the guy made him uneasy. He was scrawny and hyperactive, and Mason always had the feeling that he was up to something. He wasn't sure if he wanted to deal with Gilbert's energy so early in the day. The only thing they seemed to have in common was a love of strong coffee, and maybe he could handle Gilbert after some of that.

He climbed out of bed and pulled on a pair of boxer shorts and a T-shirt, in case Gilbert barged in early, and slinked into the kitchen to make a pot of espresso. He drank half of it sitting cross-legged on the bed with his laptop, reading email and news. Eventually he heard the doorbell. He decided Gilbert wouldn't mind that he was still wearing boxer shorts, and after a few minutes he padded down the hall and found Ned and Gilbert lounging on the sofa, coffee mugs in hand. Gilbert wore a T-shirt garishly printed in black with what looked like street-gang graffiti.

"Hey, it's the psychic investigator," Gilbert said, rising to give Mason a brief hug. "I hear you're the new master of psychic crime fighting."

"Yeah, that's about right," Mason said, sitting down on the other wing of the sofa to face them.

"Looking good, man," Gilbert said. "You're almost buff. Have you been going to the gym?"

"No," Mason said.

Ned said, "It's all the cycling. It gives your legs great musculature."

"Whatever you call it, I'd say you're stacked.

Foxy, even," Gilbert said. "And looking pretty gropable right now, I might add."

"Thanks," Mason said, slightly flustered. That was so typical of Gilbert, he thought, putting everyone off balance. "I bet you're just saying that because I'm a redhead. The fox thing, I mean. Foxes are red."

"It's because you're wearing booty shorts," Ned said, and to Gilbert, "Stop flirting with my boyfriend, you whore."

"I call 'em like I see 'em, and he is looking extremely hot today."

"Am I mistaken in thinking that you're straight, Gilbert?" Mason said. "Last time you were here, you flirted shamelessly with Peggy, and now with me. It raises several interesting questions."

"Hotness isn't limited to categories, man. Free your mind. I respond to the hotness when I see it; it's that simple."

"OK, well, I guess I'm flattered, then. What happened to your arm?" Mason asked, glad to change the subject. Gilbert's forearm was wrapped in three-inch-wide gauze taped over a bulging bandage.

"When I worked at that warehouse place they implanted me with a tracking device, so I had to fly out to Colorado to get it removed. I just got back yesterday."

"Why did you have to go to Colorado?"

"There's a guy there who specializes in removing these things. He's pretty sure he got it out; sometimes they automatically burrow deeper when you go fishing for them. But so far, so good."

Ned nodded and sipped his coffee.

Mason stared at Gilbert for a moment. "I thought it was something electronic. How can a tracking device burrow itself into your flesh? Is it a living thing, like a parasite?"

"It's definitely not alive. It's made of metals and stuff. Most of them have a high manganese content. I saw it on a scan the doctor did."

"OK, so, what kind of technology can do that, dig through your flesh?"

"Oh, I thought you knew," Gilbert said, raising his eyebrows and holding Mason's gaze. "It's alien technology."

"OK. So you've been implanted by space aliens." He looked from Gilbert to Ned, but they both looked completely serious.

"No," Gilbert said. "Didn't I just explain this? The company where I was working," he said slowly, as if to a kid with ADD, "implanted it. Right here, in my arm." He tapped his bandage.

"But they have alien technology."

"Of course." Gilbert's eyes narrowed. "What kind of earth technology could do something like burrowing autonomously through my muscles? That's crazy. No one on this planet has ever made anything like that. The only possibility is that it's alien technology. Where they got it from, I have no idea." He took a sip of his coffee and set the cup on the table.

Mason looked at Ned, who nodded again, thoughtfully. "So, you believe that Gilbert was

implanted with a burrowing tracking device created by space aliens, but you don't believe that I
can pick up psychic information from a missing
woman's necklace." He shook his head in disbelief.

"When you put it that way," Ned said, "it
sounds kind of irrational. But really, there's nothing about Gilbert's implant that contradicts what
science says about the world."

"Except that it's fucking impossible," Mason
said, perhaps too loudly.

"Dude, chill," Gilbert said. "It's out of me now,
so there's nothing to stress about."

"That's not what I'm stressing about," Mason
said sharply. "So, Gilbert, do you believe that I
might have psychic power, or do you think I'm
delusional, like Ned does?"

"Sweetie, I never said you were delusional,"
Ned said.

Gilbert said, "I suppose it's possible. We did
that séance with your hot roommate, but nothing
really happened. So I've never seen any evidence of
it, but it would be closed-minded of me to rule it
out without examining the evidence."

"Gilbert, you're the guy who told me the Roman
Catholic pope was secretly replaced by a Chinese
robot," Mason said, leaning forward. "Your mind
is already open. Wide, wide open."

"But there's clear evidence of that—proof,
really. If you watch video footage of the pope slowed
way down, it shows that his facial expressions follow the exact same sequence as these cybernetic
systems developed by a company in Guangzhou.

That company is a huge contractor for the Chinese military, so it all fits."

"I see," Mason said, leaning back and cradling his coffee cup in both hands. "I didn't realize there was such convincing irrefutable proof. It all makes sense now."

Gilbert looked puzzled. "It sounds like you don't believe it, but yeah, there's hours of video evidence. But tell me about your new job. Nedster said you went to a strip club hunting down a missing person. That sounds like my kind of career."

"Yeah, we went last night," he said, and looked briefly at Ned.

"So you had some kind of 'psychic flash,'" Gilbert said, waggling his fingers to make air quotes, "that told you to go to a strip club?"

Mason felt his cheeks redden. "Yes, Gilbert, it was just like that."

"He gets psychic flashes in dreams too," Ned said. Mason wasn't sure if he was trying to be supportive or to reinforce Gilbert's disbelief.

"Cool," Gilbert said. "How does that work?"

Mason fought the urge to roll his eyes. "Well, the other night, for instance, I dreamed I was in the Caribbean. We went to Saint Martin last year, right, so it wasn't a great psychic leap to be dreaming about it. But it was a strong, vivid image, which makes me think it was psychic information rather than just the noise of my own brain, but I don't know what it means yet."

"Was I with you in the dream?" Ned asked.

"Nope. I was walking along the beach, and

there were these Englishmen there. I'm not sure if they were English, actually, but they were dressed in English suits, on the beach. I wasn't really with them, but they were there, kind of focusing on me, maybe trying to get my attention."

"What did they look like?" Gilbert asked.

"Uh, middle-aged, beefy, happy."

"Were there four of them?"

"Yes, there were, in fact. At first just two, but then four. Why do you ask?"

"It sounds like the Epworth bankers," Gilbert said. "There were four of them. It's a seriously mysterious unsolved mystery from a few years ago. Maybe you're getting psychic information to help figure it out. Until now it's been one of those things with no solution, just tons of speculation."

"Wow, I'm flattered that you consider my psychic abilities real after all," Mason said with a broad smile. "Thanks so much for that, Gilbert. It's very validating."

"Be nice," Ned said gently. "So what's the mystery?"

"Well, it wasn't in Saint Martin, it was one of those Anglo places with banking secrecy laws and no banking oversight, like the Cayman Islands, maybe? I think the town was called Epworth, or maybe that was the name of the church. But anyway, one morning there's four of them in this little church that's like two hundred years old, and an earthquake hits. The roof falls in, and all four of them die. There's no one else in the church when they pull the bodies out of the rubble, and they don't have anything with them—no bags or anything. I think there were other people killed elsewhere on the island, but not many."

"A church?" Mason said, thinking of his second dream of the Englishmen. But there was no way he was going to share that with Gilbert. "I think I remember that earthquake. It's all very tragic, but what's the mysterious part?"

"Well, these four guys are higher-ups at four different banks in London and New York, right, busy corporate guys. Other than that, there was no reason for these four people to have known one another, much less be hanging out together. What were they doing together in an isolated little church in the middle of nowhere in the Caribbean? The official story is that they were all on vacation, but it was way too big a coincidence. They were staying at different places around the island, and they were all traveling alone. The police recovered their belongings from the hotels, but it was just regular stuff, socks and jocks and passports, nothing to show what they were really doing.

"But there was a journalist who did some digging into it because it smelled fishy. At first she was just trying to find out why a London banker became an earthquake victim, but then it's like, whoa, there were four of them, they're all bankers, but not working together, and not staying together, but they die together. What were they up to? So she digs deeper, and interviews their colleagues, and she finds anecdotal evidence that there were major loads of cash missing in deals that a couple of these guys had done. But those banks don't talk publicly about that stuff, right, because they don't want to scare their clients and investors. This journalist figured they probably stole from the banks themselves, rather than from customers, or it would have become public. Some of those transnational banks are shady outfits too, laundering drug money and all that; they'd be smart to keep it quiet."

Mason felt his excitement rising. Was there a connection? Four bankers in a rural church in the Caribbean; the story was too much like his dream to be just a coincidence.

"This wasn't more than two or three years ago," Gilbert said. "You could look it up."

"Does it sound like your dream?" Ned asked.

"Well, maybe there's a connection," Mason said, trying not to betray his rising excitement. "It's an interesting story. I don't think I have any insight into the suits, though, if they're the same people. They were just hanging around on the beach, and none of them said anything."

"I'll look it up," Ned said. "Let me get my tablet."

While he was gone, Gilbert said, "So I understand you might have a lead on your missing person. That must be exciting."

Mason felt a flash of annoyance that Ned had been gossiping about his work, which neither he nor Gilbert seemed to take seriously. But Gilbert seemed genuinely interested in what he was doing, so maybe he was just trying to connect.

"Yeah, hopefully I'll get some answers for her

mother about why she's been missing."

Ned was engrossed in his tablet when he came back into the living room. "They were in the hamlet of Epworth, more of a crossroads than a village, in the mountains on Lesser Slaughter, which is one of the British Virgin Islands." He sat down and scanned the screen. "One of them had a house here in Los Angeles, but he was based in New York." He scrolled through the article with a finger and scanned the text. "It was never clearly demonstrated that they were up to something shady, but this writer contends that they were there to stash or launder their ill-gotten funds. She thinks they were a cabal of big-league thieves who shared resources and had been getting away with it for years. Why else would they be on a tiny island like that, other than for the banking secrecy laws?"

"Who did the LA guy work for?" Mason asked.

"Uh … a Swiss bank, SMFE. That's suspicious right there."

"That bank's gone now," Gilbert said. "It collapsed in the last economic crisis. They were the preferred bank of the Mexican drug cartels, and the U.S. was going after them in the courts when the bank went under."

"Interesting stuff," Mason said. "I'm not sure if it connects to my dream, but who knows?"

"There are photos," Ned said. "Does this look like one of your dream bankers?" He swiped the screen to enlarge the images and passed the tablet over to Mason.

Ned had zoomed in on a color photo of the

ruined church. It looked nothing like his dream image, but dreams were symbolic, he reasoned, so there was no reason that it would. The next photo was a black-and-white image with the unmistakable grainy dots of an old printed newspaper. It was a portrait of one of the bankers. The vaguely double chin, the lopsided grin, probably from being surprised by the photographer, and even the overly wide pinstripes—Mason saw instantly that this was one of the guys from the beach, and one of those who had led him up the hill.

"Jesus," he said, staring at the photo, unable to conceal his excitement any longer.

"You recognize him?" Ned asked.

"You're going to think I'm crazy—crazier—but I dreamed about this guy. I was dancing with him on the beach in Saint Martin. He was the first one I saw. He was behind me, and he kind of startled me."

Ned reached for the tablet and looked at the picture. "His name is Michael Burke. I can't say I'm jealous that you were dancing with him," he said. "This guy looks like the 'before' picture for an emergency makeover." With mock passion he added, "I'm not threatened, Mason."

"I knew it," Gilbert said, slapping his knee. "Maybe you're destined to solve the mystery of the Epworth bankers."

"That sounds like a huge responsibility. I'll have to think about it. For now, though, I've got work to do." He rose to leave. "I have to get downtown, so gentlemen, let me wish you a pleasant afternoon."

"Don't leave us hanging on the bankers," Gilbert called after him. "I'll expect a full report."

MASON HADN'T WANTED TO appear too excited about the dream connection, especially since they were both being so unsupportive, but he felt elated. There was no good reason for him to be dreaming about people he'd never heard of, but at least the newspaper article showed that it really was valid extrasensory information. He was dreaming about real people, people his conscious brain didn't know about, which meant it was coming from somewhere other than his own head.

He pulled on a short-sleeved shirt and his cargo shorts and headed out, riding down the hill to the station and locking up his bike there; he only planned to go to the library, and it was close to the metro.

On the train he stared at the concrete tunnel flashing past and thought through the conversation with Gilbert and Ned. It was exhilarating to know that the dream material was something real, because it meant his attempts at lucid dreaming were working. But even if the dream imagery was extrasensory, there was really nothing that could be done with it; it was only the vaguest hint of something larger. Maybe the most logical course of action was to try to get more information in another lucid dream. Because this was something new, he reasoned, maybe it was like trying to find some distant object through a pair of binoculars. You move them around and lots of different things come into the field of view, and eventually you home in and focus on the thing you want. Hopefully he would get focused quickly.

His plan for the day had been to use the library's resources to try to find out more about Sherri, if he could, but given that her own mother had gone so far as to run her credit and couldn't find anything, he wasn't too hopeful. He found a free desk in the periodicals section, near the reference desk, and pulled out his computer. A Web search didn't turn up anything of value, so he went to the reference desk and asked to get connected to the library's digital newspaper archive. He had to fill out a request form to use it, probably because the library paid dearly for access to it, but it would be worth the effort; the archive included articles in papers from all over the world for the past twenty years.

Back at his desk, he was surprised at the number of hits he got with Sherri's name. A couple were stories about the church in a local Leimert Park newspaper, and there were items that mentioned her activities at high school. But there was nothing dated since her disappearance. He spent forty minutes digging through every subset of data he could find, even searching for alternate spellings of her name, but there was nothing. It was like she had existed one day, and not the next. The government didn't know anything about her either, at least not in Social Security records or the death rolls.

To combat his frustration, he decided to look up the Epworth bankers, to see if he might correlate them to his lucid dream in some other way.

There were dozens of Web pages that referenced them, mostly on conspiracy websites, and on sites that pilloried the banking industry and the structure of the world economy, but the basic elements were all taken from the original story that Ned had found. It had been printed eighteen months ago in the *Charlotte Scoop and Analyzer,* which Mason had never heard of. Was that a red flag? It sounded more like the name of an archaeology newsletter. He clicked through to a few other pieces written by the same journalist. She appeared to be a legitimate staff writer, and she often covered the banking industry.

The article didn't have a lot of detail about the lives of the four victims, including the one he had recognized, listed as Michael "Mickey" Burke, but rather focused on their careers in the banking industry. Burke was the only American, Mason realized, and was the one who had owned a house in LA; the other three had been from London and Amsterdam. In the newspaper archive, he ran a search for Mickey Burke. There wasn't much more to be found than what the journalist at the *Scoop and Analyzer* had reported, but there were a few more photos of the guy at public events and parties through the years.

The most recent photo was dated just a few months before the earthquake in the Caribbean; it was a group shot of an event in LA. People with money got invited to this kind of fund-raiser all the time, and one way to induce them to shell out was to create an atmosphere where they felt they shared the limelight with celebrities. There were always lots of publicity photos on mini red carpets with celebrities of varying degrees of notoriety; at his old job, Mason had seen thousands of these images. Burke was barely discernible in the crowd, as the focus of the photo was on the foreground, a fairly famous actor yapping into a microphone. Mason's first instinct was to skip over it. But he looked again, and zoomed in on Burke. Standing next to him, almost on his arm, really, was a tall woman. He felt the hair bristle on the back of his neck. Could that be Sherri Millar? She was standing in profile, wearing a summer dress to match Burke's light-colored suit, and had her hair pulled back. The hairline was right, and the skin tone. Her build looked about right, based on Miss Cassie's photo. If it was her, and there was a connection between the missing Sherri Millar and his dreams, it definitely meant his psychic powers were getting sharper.

"Like a laser beam, baby," he said aloud. The librarian at the reference desk looked up at him. Mason gave him a sheepish little wave and looked back at his screen. It could be her, he thought, but it might not be. The caption listed just a few of the key figures in the image, including "Mickey Burke, SMFE Global Markets," with no mention of the woman beside him. He looked up other images from the event, but there were none with Burke or the woman in them. She also wasn't in any of the older photos with Burke. He went back to the image and zoomed in and out, trying to make up his mind. He saved a copy of it so that he could look at it again later. Whether it was her or not, he decided, the thing to do was to wait for her to call—or go back to see Champagne, which he really didn't want to do.

He logged out of the archive, then sat and thought for a moment. If dreams were mostly symbolic, maybe he could get a clue from their details. He did a Web search for "stone church," then "fieldstone church," and then "church on a hill," and waded through the results. Nothing stood out as significant or triggered other associations. He searched for "stone wall" and then "wall of stones." That was a hit: he found that in Celtic mythology, the wall of stones represented the line between the world of the living and the world of the dead. That was where the suits in his dream had gone, across the wall of stones into the dark. And he had known instinctively that he couldn't go there himself.

He wasn't sure he wanted to share these discoveries with Ned, or anyone else, not yet. If Sherri Millar really was the woman in that photo with an Epworth banker, it was a huge lead, but he still wasn't sure of that. In any case, if he headed out now, he'd be in time to have dinner at home.

NED GREETED HIM FROM the kitchen when he walked into the house. He was wearing an apron and rapidly dicing tomatoes.

"I'm loving the summer of tomatoes," Mason said, sliding onto a barstool and setting his backpack on the floor. "What are you going to do with those?"

"I'm thinking bruschetta, only scaled up in size so that it's a whole meal. Maybe a salad on the side."

"That sounds amazing."

"Peggy won't be home until later, so it's just you and me."

"Did Gilbert stay long?"

"Long enough for me to make him lunch, and then I had to get back to work."

"So is he actually bisexual, or was he just trying to unnerve me?" Mason asked. "I wanted to go have a shower to wash it off."

"I think he's just very sexual. I don't think he sleeps with guys, really, but I don't know that for sure."

"How could you not know that about a close friend? It seems kind of fundamental."

"We're old friends, and all that stuff came along later for both of us. I'm not concerned with that part of his life."

"Even when he flirts with everyone you know?"

"It's kind of endearing, isn't it? I don't think he actually sleeps around a lot. And he doesn't mean anything by it," Ned said.

"Except that he's presenting as a ho bag. I think he did it because he thinks I'm square and he wanted to make me blush."

"You are square, I'm afraid, but you're pretty when you blush. Like a fresh ripe tomato. I think he did it because he thought you were dressed provocatively, and you do have nice legs."

"I guess I earned it, then, for dressing all slutty." Mason sighed.

"How was your research trip?" Ned asked, dousing the tomatoes with olive oil.

"It went all right, I guess," Mason said. "I don't think I'm any wiser than I was this morning." It wasn't really a lie, he reasoned, because he hadn't found anything concrete, just possibilities. Mostly he just didn't want to deal with Ned's skepticism right now. "The next thing is to talk to the missing woman herself, hopefully, if Champagne can make that happen."

"What about the bankers?" he asked. "Did you look into that?"

"I will at some point. I think I need to focus on the paying jobs first."

MASON'S PHONE RANG SOON after they had sat down to eat. He pulled it out of his pocket. "It's a blocked number," he said. "I'm not answering it. It's probably telemarketers. Who else calls at dinnertime?"

"Mason, think! What if it's your stripper friend?"

"She said it would take her a couple of days." But maybe Ned was right, he thought, and he answered it "Braithwaite."

"Who is this?" a woman's voice said.

"I've got a better one for you, sister. You called me—who are you?" But he already knew. When he heard her voice, a flash of insight told him it was Sherri. He set down his fork and went out on the balcony to focus on the call.

"I understand you were looking for someone last night in Hollywood. What is it exactly that you want with her?"

"Well, if 'her' is you, and you're Sherri Millar, I'm working for your mother. She's concerned that you haven't contacted her for so long, and she'd like to know that you're OK."

"No," she said, "I know that's not true. She wouldn't try to find me. If she had wanted to, she would have done it years ago. Let's try again. Who are you, and why are you snooping around in my business?"

"My name is Mason. You're right; it's true that your mother wasn't anxious to have me look for you. That doesn't mean she doesn't think about you, though. There were other people at St. Agatha's who were worried about you when you left. To them you just disappeared, and no one knew what had happened. Mrs. Lewis thought you might even be dead."

There was a long pause. "That also doesn't sound quite right. Nobody at St. Agatha's would come looking for me after all this time. Perhaps you met them in the course of working for one of my business associates."

"It may sound strange, but it's the truth. And there's no one else. Champagne should have told you that I wasn't one of your former cohorts."

"All Champagne told me was that some stumblebum came into her place of employment looking for me. And what do you know of my cohorts?"

"Did she actually call me that?"

"Her very words."

"Nice. Listen, I don't really know anything about you, just tidbits here and there, and what your mom and Betty Lewis told me. And that's fine by me. Really, personally, I don't care whether you're dead or alive. But I did some other research work for St. Agatha's, and they were concerned about you, and they asked me to look for you. They want to find out if you're all right, because no one has heard anything about you for years. I don't think they expected you to disappear for good."

Another pause; Mason assumed she was deciding whether to believe him or not. "Well, I guess you can report back that I'm alive and well, and that can be the end of it."

"I'd like to meet with you," he said quickly. "Just to be sure you are who you say you are."

"That's not possible."

"Just for a few minutes, Sherri. Then I'll leave you alone. I'm not going to ask you to go back there or meet with anyone. It's just to verify. Anyway, I've already found you, when it seems you worked pretty hard not to be found."

"That actually is surprising. But I really don't think a meeting is a good idea."

"I'm also curious about Mickey. Losing him must have been devastating." He waited, gripping the balcony rail with his free hand, but she said nothing. He was taking a risk; if he was wrong about her being connected to the Epworth bankers, she would never agree to meet him.

Finally, she said, "I don't know what you're talking about."

He knew she was lying. Her tone had changed; it was either an emotional topic, or she was shocked that Mason knew about the connection. So it really had been her in the photo. He could feel his heart pounding. "Yeah, I think you do, Sherri," he said, perhaps more forcefully than he had intended.

"Mason, you said your name was."

"Yes."

"Mason, what are you looking for, exactly? Why are you messing in my business?"

"I already explained that," he said. "And I'll stop messing in your business after we have a face-to-face. Just for a few minutes, Sherri, and then I'll let it go."

"And if not, I suppose you'll just keep digging."

"That's the implication, yes."

"Hmm," she said. "Tomorrow, then. One o'clock."

"So you're nearby," he said.

"One o'clock," she said, her voice terse now. "Do you know Niçoise on Robertson?"

"I'm sure I can find it. It's a café?"

"A bistro, actually. And come alone."

"That sounds ominous," he said.

"If you really are working for St. Agatha's or for my mother, I don't want you to bring any of them. Or anyone else. Just you and me in a neutral public place."

"That I can do."

"Until then," she said, and hung up.

He put his phone back in his pocket and went back inside. Ned was eating and watching him expectantly.

"Was it really her?" Ned asked.

"I think so, yeah."

"Who's Mickey?"

"Long story. Champagne definitely did contact her, though. That phony blond told her I was a stumblebum."

"But she just met you for a couple of minutes. How could she know that you're a stumblebum?"

"I know, right?"

"Mason, you actually found her."

"I think so. She agreed to meet with me tomorrow. I'm not sure she completely buys that I'm working for her mother and Mrs. Lewis, but I'm pretty sure it was her."

"I guess you'll find out tomorrow. But as you said, she really didn't want to be found, so she'll probably try to get you to lay off and leave her alone. You're meeting her in a café? It's a public place, I hope?"

"Yes, at a bistro. I think that was her idea too, to be in a public place with witnesses in case I have any sinister intentions."

"What bistro?" He pushed his empty plate away as Mason started on his.

"Some place over on Robertson. I hate going over there. It's so pretentious, and far from the train."

"You want me to come with you?"

"No, she asked me to come alone. It makes sense—she doesn't want to deal with her mother, or with any unknowns."

"But you feel safe meeting her? I'm still thinking about the shoe-store guy and the mention of thieves."

"She has no idea who I really am, but she was willing to talk, so I don't think she's that dangerous."

"So what did she sound like?" Ned asked.

"She didn't sound drug-addled or angry. And now that I think about it, she sounded kind of polished, or maybe even pretentious. It fits with what her mother said about her being a social climber. Her dialect is completely different from Miss Cassie's too, like an old-money dialect or something."

"That would be something new for the stripper who traded blow jobs for shoes."

"Come on, man. How do you think half the people dining out on Robertson got to be dining out on Robertson?" They both laughed.

"Of anywhere in the country, LA is definitely the place where social classes are most flexible," Ned said. "Everyone's new here because it's a new place, and you really can reinvent yourself if you have the resources. I bet that if she were still a stripper, she wouldn't have chosen to meet you at a bistro on Robertson."

"Right."

Mason cleared away their dishes, and Ned went down the hall to "read or watch the news, not necessarily in that order." Mason was still in the kitchen when Peggy got home.

"Guess who called?" he asked her when she greeted him.

"No way! Your missing woman?"

"Just a few minutes ago."

"Mason, that's great." She sat at one of the

barstools. "Is there any dinner left? I haven't eaten."

"Bruschetta by Chef Edgar. He set aside some for you," he said, pulling the plastic wrap off the plate and sliding it across the bar to her.

"This looks amazing. So what did your mystery woman have to say?"

"I'm going to meet her. She didn't want to at first, but I nudged her into it."

"Right on," she said, biting into the bruschetta.

"And Champagne told her I was a stumble-bum."

"But she just met you. How could she characterize you as a stumblebum after one brief lap dance?"

"I guess I make a less-than-suave first impression. But the upside is that Sherri did call me, and I'm going to meet her tomorrow. If it really is her, that is. But I think it is."

"Damn, Mason, you're getting good at this," she said.

"Bizarre, right? I'm not even sure how I'm doing it."

"I'm surprised that you're surprised. Wasn't this all part of your plan?"

"Yes, it was. But Ned still thinks it's totally bogus, of course, and so does Gilbert, and Miss Cassie too. But I know it's real. I guess I'm just not used to … being so successful."

"You got a psychic lead from a piece of jewelry, and then it panned out. Ned's blind if he doesn't believe that. It's undeniable—you've got the power."

"Remember the Magic 8 Ball when you were a

kid? One of the answers it gave was 'Signs point to yes.' That's what I'd say about this new venture—signs point to yes."

Friday

I**T WAS A LONG** trip to where Sherri wanted to meet, and it took Mason half the morning to sort out the logistics of getting over there. He had decided to cycle, even though that meant he'd be sweaty when he got there. He knew he had to dress up a little, as the café's address indicated it was surely upscale. He thought about all this as he made coffee, and after downing his second pot with his muesli and a couple of peaches, he got dressed. The only way to look presentable after a long bike ride was to wear an undershirt. Over it he put on a light shirt that would stay fairly dry, and dark shorts that could pass for hot-weather semiformal. The shoes were easy; he wore his bright-orange skater shoes, which were comfortable to walk and cycle in but were odd-looking enough that, he hoped, they looked alternative and creative, which passed for formality in LA.

More than an hour before he was due to meet Sherri, he rode down the hill to the boulevard, where he could catch an express bus to take him part of the way. Luckily there was a space on the first bus's bike rack. He secured his bike, boarded, and stared out the window as the city rolled by. It had been a gamble dropping the banker's name with Sherri, but whether it was the reason she had agreed to meet him or not, he seemed to have struck a nerve. Hopefully she would explain why. And depending on what he could take back to Miss Cassie and Mrs. Lewis, he thought, he might even earn some money. Thinking about what had happened in the past few days, it was remarkable that he'd come so far.

He realized he was nervous about meeting her. He'd been feeling resentful at having to schlep across town to an inconvenient neighborhood, but when he really thought about it, beneath that was fear. It was so predictable, he thought. Fear was under so much of the way he reacted to the world. He really didn't know anything about her, and the worst possibility was that she was still involved with thieves, besides her dead-banker party escort. He spent a few minutes with his eyes closed, trying to calm his mind.

Soon enough he had to get off the bus, grab his bike, and cycle the last mile or so. Riding on the streets was perilous, with the death rate for cyclists hit by cars in Southern California averaging one a day in the summer. But he stuck to back streets that he knew had fewer driveways, and he wore his helmet. The key was to anticipate what the cars were going to do; they almost always acted predictably, if not legally or morally.

He locked his bike to a street sign half a block from the café. He looped the chain lock through his helmet so that he could go in without it, but he kept his backpack on. It was quarter to one, so he'd be able to get comfortable before Sherri arrived.

Niçoise lived up to the pretense that its name implied. Even the busboys wore black and white, and there were a lot of them, always a sign of an upscale eatery. The tables inside were spaced well apart, most of them occupied, and the high-backed booths around the walls had curtains to shut out the rest of the room. It would be easy to spend time here and go unseen; perhaps that was what the clientele wanted.

"For one?" the maître d' asked, smiling and friendly but quickly glancing at his shorts and the orange sneakers. He was probably wondering if Mason was someone important, Mason realized.

"I'm actually meeting someone," Mason said. "Is there a table out front?" He knew there were a few open, as he had just walked past them.

"Right this way." There were lots of other people dining on the patio, but he showed Mason to a quiet table. The patio was elevated and set back from the street behind some fragmented shrubbery that still allowed a view of people walking by. He sat down and looked around, planning his escape route; he could vault over a three-foot-high railing less than twenty feet away without trampling anyone, and he'd land on the sidewalk. It was probably an extreme idea, and Sherri had almost certainly picked this place because she was equally worried about his motives, but he wanted to be prepared for anything. He set his backpack beside his chair within easy grab-and-run reach and breathed deeply a few times, trying to calm down.

A waiter in a white shirt and a bowtie appeared. Career waiter, Mason thought, another sign of upscale dining.

"Something to drink?" he asked.

"Can you make me a quadruple espresso?"

"Of course," he said, and was gone.

Mason nervously watched the podium by the maître d, and just as his coffee arrived, he saw her. It was Sherri, unmistakably, but she had an aura that wasn't evident in the old photos of her. It might have been the effect of money, he thought, but it was more than that. She had a presence, taking up more space and drawing more attention than an ordinary person. She spoke briefly to the maître d' and glanced around inside the restaurant. When Mason realized she didn't know what he looked like and wouldn't be able to recognize him, he exhaled deeply to counter the surge of adrenaline, and waved at her. The maître d' saw him instantly and smiled, and led her toward Mason. As she walked over, her expression was impassive, her eyes hidden behind massive sunglasses. She was wearing a flowy dress with brilliant shimmering birds of paradise printed on it. Judging by the look of it and the way it fit her figure, it had to be couture. Despite the heat she had a tiny pink Grace Kelly sweater-jacket over her shoulders. Her hair was pulled back in myriad small braids, a subtle but ornate gold pin holding them in place.

"Hello," Mason said, and stood awkwardly, bumping the table and sloshing some of his coffee into its saucer. He didn't extend his hand; it didn't seem appropriate. Instead he stood there and grinned and tried not to gape.

"Mason, I presume?" she said.

"Yes. It's nice to finally meet you, Sherri. You've changed a lot from the photos I saw at St. Agatha's."

"I don't use that name anymore," she said, but didn't offer another option. She sat down when the maître d' pulled out the chair for her, and Mason sat too.

Her presence reminded him of an encounter he'd had years ago in Ghana. He was sitting in a public hall waiting for a fashion show to begin. He was just a tourist, but for Accra's elite it was an important event in the social calendar. A woman came to take a seat in the row in front of him, dressed in strikingly beautiful robes and dripping with gold jewelry. The seat was dusty, like everything was in the dry season, so she hesitated to sit down. As she looked around, perhaps for an usher or someone with a cloth, Mason had pulled out his handkerchief and quickly wiped the dust off her seat. She gave him a most intense and meaningful look and said simply, "Thank you." That look, and the weight of those words, were something he'd never seen in the West, so powerful and elegant and graceful. They came from a place of lifelong privilege developed over generations, he was sure, and being dazzled by it for a moment was more than sufficient reward for the simple thing he'd done for her. That was the energy Sherri was emanating: privileged elegance. Even the waiter seemed mesmerized as he took her drink order.

"A gimlet, with Tanqueray," she said, her face turned slightly down rather than toward the waiter, as if it were a difficult or embarrassing thing to say.

California is so new that the wealthy are usually pretty down to earth, but somehow in just a few years Sherri had developed a moneyed aura that Mason had only ever seen in the Old World. But he had issues with social class, and no intention of being in her thrall.

"So you're the guy," she said, leaning slightly forward. "Champagne told me you were too soft to be a cop or a Fed. I would have to agree with that assessment."

He nodded. "She also told me that she didn't think I was one of your criminal associates."

"And I would agree with that as well," she said, not missing a beat. "Criminals usually aren't quite so ... square." She said it as gently as possible, as if wanting to be truthful but not critical.

"I guess that's flattering. I'm happy not to look like a crook." He could feel his cheeks reddening.

"Mobsters typically have scars and broken noses, that kind of thing," she explained. "Your nose is lovely and straight. It's a dead giveaway." She was silent for a few moments, sizing him up further from behind her dark glasses. "So you're not a mobster, and you're not the authorities. Once again the question becomes—" She broke off as the waiter set down her cocktail, and she waited for him to leave. "Who are you, and what do you want?"

"Well, it's exactly like I said on the phone. I'm an investigator, and I did some work for St. Agatha's. I helped them solve a problem they were having, and they were quite happy with my work. Mrs. Lewis was the one who suggested that I use my skills to try to find out what had become of you."

"And so this is a shakedown, then? If I pay you to leave me alone, you'll leave me alone, something along those lines."

"What? No." He set his coffee cup down abruptly, and it rattled on its saucer. Despite her cool presentation, he thought, maybe she was actually afraid of him. He wished she'd take off those damn sunglasses so he could get a better read.

"Blackmail, I suspect, becomes frustrating for the victim," she said. "The question eventually becomes whether to pay, or whether to eliminate the source of the problem. I'm sure more than one blackmailer has ended up in a shallow grave."

"Jesus," he said, alarmed. "It's nothing like that. I'm getting paid by Mrs. Lewis. Now that I've seen it's really you, I can go back to them and tell them you're just fine, living the high life on the Westside, or wherever, and I'll get paid. All they wanted to know was that you're not dead, that you're missing from their lives by choice." He looked at her for a moment, trying to decide if she really was threatening him. "You know, Mrs. Lewis said something just like that—she wondered if you had somehow wound up in a shallow grave out in the desert."

"So vivid. That does sound like her," she said.

"I just needed to make sure it was really you. I'm verifying what I've found out through my research, nothing more than that." He took a sip of coffee, and Sherri remained silent. "I don't even know enough about your criminal activities or your relationship with Mickey to blackmail you with. And even if I did know anything, I wouldn't do that. As strange as it might sound to you, I don't want your money."

Sherri smiled and sipped her cocktail. She set it down again and laughed softly.

"You don't believe me," Mason said, relieved to hear her laugh after her veiled threat.

"I find it hard to believe that your motives are so simple."

"You think I'm a chump for not maximizing my payout."

"If you're willing to work for what Betty Lewis will be able to pay you, good for you," she said. "It's all right. Don't get agitated." She finally pulled off her sunglasses and looked at him. Her eyes were much softer than he had expected.

The waiter appeared and asked, "Something to eat?"

"I bet my mother loves you," she said to Mason, ignoring the waiter. Then, turning to him, she said, "A small garden salad, with oil and vinegar."

"Uh … I'll have the same," Mason said, "and make sure there's no cheese on it. And another coffee."

"Very good," he said, and was gone.

Mason hadn't really been prepared for this. She didn't seem dangerous, even though she had possibly just threatened his life, but it seemed weird that they were going to have lunch together.

"So your motivations are altruistic," she said. "I guess I can accept that. It's quaint."

"I'm not being altruistic at all. I'm getting paid, and not trying to shake you down is actually completely selfish. I need to be able to live with myself and not feel guilty about what I do."

"As I said, quaint. But what I really want to know is how you connected me with Mickey, and how you connected Champagne with Sherri from St. Agatha's. That's really the only reason I'm sitting here. You seem to know a lot."

"I have lots of questions for you too. If I answer yours, maybe you can answer mine."

She dropped her chin and looked up at him, wide-eyed. "My," she said, "it's like a negotiation." She was almost flirting, he realized. He wondered fleetingly whether that stuff really had an effect on straight guys. Women probably wouldn't bother if it didn't work some of the time.

"I'm fairly new at this kind of work," he began. "The St. Agatha's job was my first contract, and it worked out really well. In the course of that job I got to know your mother a little, and I met Mrs. Lewis too. She had me over for lemonade."

"I bet you needed dental work after that. Her lemonade should be illegal."

"I know," he said, smiling and leaning forward. "I was afraid to try the cookies." He leaned back again. "Anyway, the idea of a missing person seemed intriguing, and I thought it would be a good challenge. And to be honest, your mother wasn't really in favor of the idea. I kind of talked her into it."

"Oh, honey, you don't have to sugarcoat it for me," she said, gesturing languidly. "I can imagine exactly how it went down. I've known that woman all my life, remember? My mother didn't want to find me, but then she gave in to placate Betty Lewis. And my mother would have made it a condition that you not put us back in communication."

Mason stared at her for a moment. "You're very shrewd," he said.

"Thank you," she said, her eyes coyly on the table, but then she looked up at him intently and said quietly, "But the key question remains unanswered. I put an awful lot of effort into making a clean break from that life. How did you find me?"

"Well, I'm not going to reveal all my methods and sources, but let's just say I got very, very lucky. If I tell you more, will you tell me how you're connected to Mickey Burke? Just to help me put the pieces together."

"I thought you knew," she said. "But I may tell you more if I buy your story."

"Deal." He grinned. "OK, so, some research and inspiration led me to a shoe store on Cahuenga and a guy named Carlos."

"Oh." She stirred her cocktail but didn't betray any surprise or discomfort. "How is Carlos these days?"

"I guess he's fine. He still works at the shoe store. I think he's a bit of a thug, though, because he chased me up the street."

Sherri laughed. "Oh, Carlos. He's so emotional."

"He pointed me to Champagne at the Toy Box, who pointed me to you. It's really that simple."

"I didn't know Carlos knew I worked there." She thought for a moment. "Hmm. And I should have schooled Champagne more effectively in not being intimidated by people who came looking for me. I never anticipated that anyone would, of course, but it seems she gave me up pretty easily, considering everything I did for her. I taught her the ropes and set her up in that job. I even gave her my name and my wig."

So Ned was right about the hair, Mason thought.

"How were you able to convince her to call me?" she asked.

"Every person that I've run across since I started looking for you has either been afraid of you, afraid of the cops, or afraid of your friends. I think that when all that fear is swirling around, it's pretty easy to motivate people. Carlos and Champagne both implied that you hung around with dangerous people, which I thought meant gangsters, but maybe they were talking about Mickey Burke."

She smiled and nodded. "I had other friends before Mickey, and that's who they would have been thinking of. My, it does sound awfully melodramatic."

"Yes, it does," Mason said emphatically. "Which brings us to my questions for you. Why the complete break from your old life? What are you mixed up in? How did Mickey Burke fit into it? And how did you get from working the swing shift at the Toy Box to lunching at Niçoise?"

At that moment the waiter presented their salads, setting them down with a flourish. "Your coffee will be right up," he said. "Another gimlet, ma'am?"

"I think I'd better, yes," she said, and laughed, fanning her face with her fingers in mock distress. Turning back to Mason, she said, "I'm not going to answer all that. You're not here for a shakedown, but I'm not going to give you reason to change your mind."

"Well, all I can say is, again, I don't even know who you are now, so no matter what you tell me, there's not even a way for me to find you again. I'm certain Champagne won't be relaying any more of my messages."

"Indeed," she said.

"I hope I haven't put her in any danger."

"No, silly boy. She was my friend." She reached over and gently tapped the back of his hand in admonishment. "I probably should have let go of that relationship along with the people in Leimert Park."

Mason nodded. "Without her, I probably wouldn't have found you."

"She thought she was protecting me by putting me in touch with you, so she's done nothing wrong." Sherri studied him for a moment. "Did anyone ever tell you that you have an earnest face?"

He wasn't sure if she was being sincere, or if it was more of the coquette. "I suppose I've heard that before, yes," he said cautiously.

"Well, you do. You're just so … pink. Your cheeks are like a lie detector."

"It was worse when I was younger," he said. "Your mother said I looked freshly boiled."

"Which reminds me," she continued. "How much of what you've learned about me are you going to tell my mother? What have you told them already? As you might imagine, I'm quite content with the status quo."

He sighed and put his fork down, thinking about how to frame the answer that he'd already come up with. "You know, I like those two at St. Agatha's. They're funny, and they're dedicated to their community. They really seem to run the show there."

"They do."

"I respect them, so I don't think I'd want to go back to them with anything that would cause them grief. I haven't told them anything yet, and my thinking right now is to omit the stuff about Carlos, and the Toy Box, and Mickey Burke. I guess I'll tell them that you're alive and doing fine, but you just don't want to be contacted."

"Very good," she said, and smiled. "And because your motivation is integrity, rather than money, I trust you'll keep your word on that. Perhaps you're more than St. Agatha's patsy after all."

"I know that you must have good reasons for keeping your past in the past, and I have no reason to cause you grief."

"You're right, I do have good reasons, and you're right that I'm not going to tell you everything. But you've done so well at digging up what I thought I had effectively buried. I think we need to talk more about that."

"As long as it doesn't mean I wind up in a shallow grave out in the desert," Mason said, only half kidding. "And, wait, you owe me one. Let's start with the break from your old life."

She laughed and shook her head. "You've met my mother, so you know how crazy she is. The best thing I could do for my own mental health was to make a complete break."

"She's a little odd, yes. But it seems extreme to cut her off completely and disappear. I mean, we're mammals. Our mother is the person we're most closely bonded to, right? You can't just switch that off."

"That sounds like something she would say. Have you been in therapy with her?"

"Oh, god, no."

"When I say she's crazy, I mean crazy. She became a psychologist to try to resolve her own mental problems. But you know, it just didn't work." As her voice rose slightly, Mason could hear the old South LA dialect creeping back. "When I was fourteen years old, she thought I had repressed anger, and she made me cry for thirty minutes a day. She stood there in my room until I did it. Can you imagine doing that to someone just starting adolescence?"

"That does sound excessive." He looked up from his salad to meet her eye.

"And she drove my father away with the craziness when I was still small. I think he was probably a good man, but I wouldn't know because I didn't manage to maintain a relationship with him, mostly because of her interference. Here's another one: at Christmas she'd have me pick out my favorite gift, and that's the one she would take away and give to a children's shelter. She said she was trying to teach me to have realistic expectations."

"Ouch. That is pretty crazy. But why the complete abandonment of your identity?" he asked, picking up his fresh coffee cup as the waiter set it down along with Sherri's second gimlet.

"You already know the answer to that," she said, sipping her drink. "Mickey Burke."

"Was he your boyfriend?"

"In a way, yes. I met Mickey when I was working at the Toy Box. I wasn't there for long after I met him. He swept me off my feet. But no one knew, not even Champagne. She knew there was a man, but not his name, and she never met him. So I know she didn't tell you about him. How did you make the connection?"

"Oh, like I said, inspiration and research," he said.

"Mason," she said, frowning and holding his gaze, "I've been quite open with you. I think you owe me the same courtesy. The only reason I'm here with you today is that my personal security is based on no one knowing that I was ever connected to Mickey Burke. If you know, I'm concerned that someone else will find out the same way. I know it wasn't Carlos or Champagne, because they never knew. So I'm quite set on you telling me the truth."

"OK," he said. "I can understand that. Finding you with him was a coincidence. A friend of mine told me the story of the Epworth bankers, which he presented as an unsolved mystery. I was curious about it, and I went to the library and read what I could find about those guys, including Mickey. Coincidentally, I was looking for you at the same time." He knew that telling her about his psychic insights would make her trust him even less. "There's a photograph of you standing beside him at a fund-raiser here in town a few years ago. It's not a good image of you, because you're far from the camera, off in the background. I wasn't even sure it was you until I talked to you on the phone."

"A photo. That's not good news."

"Well, it was just the one; believe me, I looked for more. And it's not on the Web. It's hidden behind a newspaper archive pay wall. The caption has his name but not yours. So unless someone already knew what you looked like, and used the archive to look at every available old photo of Mickey, they would never be able to find the connection. It could be any random woman standing beside him;

it's not even obvious that you're together."

"OK."

"So honestly, I think you're safe. It was a complete fluke that I found you in that photo."

"Let's hope that you, my dear, are the only one who could have done that."

"So why does your safety depend on not being connected to him? Didn't any of his cohorts know you?"

"No, they didn't. I knew that Mickey was involved in some unsavory ventures. I had nothing to do with any of that, of course," she said, and waved her hand dismissively. "I knew I'd be better off not mixed up in that part of his life. He loved me, and he took care of me, and that was enough. And when that earthquake struck, it was tragic bad timing for Mickey, but for me, something magical happened. You could say I was in the right place at the right time."

"You were with him on the island?"

She sighed. Mason realized she was hesitant to say more, but she continued. "Yes. Mickey had converted the bulk of their offshore earnings into untraceable financial assets. I didn't know that at the time," she said, "but the point is, I was back at the villa he had rented in the town, while he was with his cohorts in that little church. I didn't know what I had until later, and I don't know why he left it with me that day, except that perhaps he didn't completely trust them. I think they were probably planning to sort out what to do with the money, and that was why they were meeting on the island.

After the earthquake, things were chaotic. I knew where he'd gone, and I walked up to the church. When I saw the rubble, I just knew he wasn't coming back. So I left his clothes at the villa, but I took my own and everything else that might have had any value. I thought I was destitute without him, you see, and wouldn't be able to leave the island without selling my jewelry or something."

"But all their money became your money." It explained her demeanor, Mason thought; if she'd suddenly become wealthy, she could have purchased her new dialect and bearing as easily as most people bought clothes. "But you're concerned someone else might come looking for it. No one ever has?" he asked. "A cohort who wasn't there that day, maybe, or someone who knew about it?"

"If they did, there was no way to link it to me. They might have looked for Sherri, but I don't think her connection to Mickey was ever really known. Mickey was careful to book our flights separately when we traveled, and he never put my name on a hotel room or anything like that. He would introduce me to people using made-up names, but rarely to his friends, and never to his business associates. He isolated me from his life. It was the way it had to be to protect himself. I could have made him vulnerable in his, uh, financial dealings."

"And once he was gone, you got rid of Sherri."

"I spent some time in the Caribbean, establishing a new identity. I purchased it, really. Sherri Millar couldn't just show up back here with all that money."

She seemed to be enjoying this, talking so frankly, he realized. She wouldn't have had many chances to divulge details of her time with Mickey, and her success in the aftermath, so maybe this was a rare opportunity for her to revel in it.

"So there's clearly no way you could have planned this, or had a hand in Mickey's demise," Mason said, watching her reaction carefully.

She didn't flinch or even blink. "No, my dear. Who could have planned for an act of God? It was just an unexpected series of events. He did love me, so it isn't even really unjust that I should inherit his money."

"So why are you here now? In LA, I mean. I'm assuming you're living around here, if you didn't fly in this morning."

"I could have gone anywhere, become anyone, it's true. But there's just something about LA. There's so much potential for new ideas, new beginnings. I think it's why people move here from everywhere else." She sipped her cocktail.

"New beginnings," Mason said. "I understand that. And the wealthy fit in easily here too. They don't look that different from everyone else. There's not enough history here for that to have happened yet. But aren't you afraid of running into people from your old life?"

"It's not likely to happen. More people live in this city than in most of the states, or any of those Caribbean islands. And the people from that time in my life, we travel in different circles."

He nodded. "So how much money?"

"Quite a lot." She raised her eyebrows. "Enough to keep me in this lifestyle forever."

"Nice. I don't suppose there's any point asking about your new name, or where you live, what you do, who you're dating."

"No."

"That makes it easier, in a way. It'll be more like the truth when I tell your mother and Mrs. Lewis that I don't have any details."

"Exactly."

He looked at her for a few moments. "You're not who I thought you were," he said. "I've heard so many different stories from different people. But I suspect you're not what any of them think you are."

"That, I will take as a compliment. You're not what I expected either. Cheers." She clinked her cocktail glass on his coffee cup, and he watched her as she nibbled on her salad.

Mason felt lighter. It was satisfying to cut through the mystery and resolve some of the unknowns. Hearing her story made her real, and despite her extraordinary circumstances, he saw that she was just another person navigating the world. It took the fear out of it for him. And it seemed he had built a little trust with her, which made them both feel safer.

"You know, Mason, there have always been people in the world with unlimited resources. It's a whole other way of life that most people don't even know about, or at most have a limited understanding of. Have you ever been to Newport? On the East Coast, I mean, Newport, Rhode Island."

He shook his head.

"There are mansions there, rows of them, from the nineteenth century, built by the wealthiest people in the country when most people lived in squalor, sleeping three to a bed. The wealthy would send their children abroad for months at a time, for the whole summer, to visit the ruins of antiquity around the Mediterranean. For most people in those days, the Old World was either a distant memory or far removed from their reality, like a fairy tale, not a place to spend the summer. I was always keenly aware of that kind of experience, and how I was missing out. I'm not sure why. I was always on the outside looking in. But now I'm one of those people."

He didn't say anything, but he nodded. She was being candid, and it explained a lot about her—more, he was sure, than she had planned to tell him. Maybe the second gimlet had lowered her guard a little. She put her fork on the salad plate, and placed her napkin beside it. He knew she wasn't going to say anything more of consequence.

Almost the moment she set her fork down, a busboy deftly took away their plates.

"Well, I must say it has been a unique pleasure," Mason said. "But I sincerely doubt that I'll ever see you again."

"It's unlikely. But I have your number. And before you go, I have to ask: as a man of integrity, will you give me your word that you'll keep my secrets?"

"I promise," he said, and grinned at her. He

pulled his wad of cash out of his pocket and peeled off a twenty. "I wonder what a salad costs in this place?"

"Oh, Mason, no," she said, and smiled. "Lunch is on me. It's the very least I can do." For just a moment she sounded like Miss Cassie.

"Thanks," he said, stuffing the twenty back as he stood up. "And I wish you luck in ... whatever it is that you do."

She laughed and nodded, and as he pulled on his backpack she extended her hand, palm down and fingers drooping like it was the 1950s, or a royal audience; he gave them a delicate squeeze.

"Good-bye, then," he said, and made his way among the tables to the sidewalk.

His bicycle was where he'd left it. He thought about riding back to a boulevard with a good bus line, but then decided just to cycle all the way home. It would take a while, but the streets were already starting to get congested, so riding around the traffic would be just as fast as sitting in it.

Sherri, or whatever she called herself now, was nothing like the dangerous criminal he had imagined she might be, he thought as he pedaled along. She had been suspicious of him at first too, but when she realized he wasn't a threat, she seemed to relax and even enjoy the conversation. She was skilled at masking her reactions, he thought, but he also decided that he believed the story about how she had become wealthy, at least in the broad strokes she had described. Whoever Mickey had been, thief or otherwise, she hadn't denied that he was a criminal or that she had subsequently acquired his ill-gotten assets. She obviously wasn't afraid of Mason, which meant she must have believed him too. It followed that he had no reason to be afraid of her either.

It made sense that Sherri couldn't have come back into the country with a stack of unexplained cash, but if she had a foreign passport, it wouldn't be suspicious at all, or even noticed, if she kept the money abroad. And if she'd been living the high life for this long, it seemed unlikely that whatever entity it had originally been stolen from would ever connect her to it. He had no idea how international banking and finance worked, but logically it would be possible to make money untraceable. If the drug cartels could do business through legitimate banks with impunity, a relatively small fish like Sherri should be able to stroll through a tax haven unnoticed.

He knew that not telling Miss Cassie and Mrs. Lewis everything he had learned was the right thing to do. They would have to take it on faith that he had found her alive and well. The worst thing that could happen is that they didn't pay him, which wasn't the end of the world, as he was really only out fifty bucks for a truncated lap dance. He hadn't had time to clear that expense with Mrs. Lewis when it came up, as requested, but it was hardly the kind of thing he would have told her about anyway. He had barely started on this career path, he reasoned, and there would be many more opportunities to make money later. It was odd to be worried about fifty dollars, he thought, when he had just had an audience with someone of unlimited means.

Having met her now, he couldn't really understand the falling out between Sherri and Miss Cassie. They both had strong personalities, and there were a lot of hard feelings on both sides, but neither one seemed completely unreasonable. He'd had that experience before with other women, a complex state of animosity between them that he couldn't really fathom. The truth about who Sherri was, and who Miss Cassie was, probably lay somewhere in between the way they'd described each other and what he could ascertain from talking with them. Miss Cassie didn't seem all that crazy, but then again, she was a shrink. Sherri didn't seem overly materialistic and superficial, but she had acquired enough money to last forever, in her own words, and she had somehow developed a regal persona; maybe she simply didn't have to be materialistic anymore. The difference between successful actors and all the wannabes floating around LA was like that: the ones who had jobs and income were pretty much like everyone else, and they made reasonable dinner guests, but the hungry ones were an off-putting jumble of insecurity and puffery that inevitably expanded to fill any space, dining room or otherwise. Maybe Sherri had simply made it, achieved what she wanted, and her personality had evened out. Their falling out really wasn't his business, he decided, and it was up to Sherri if she wanted to work on it someday; he doubted Miss Cassie would be able to find her if she ever decided she wanted to try to patch things up.

Cycling the last half mile up the hill to their house was always the least enjoyable part of any excursion, but he'd done it regularly enough that he could get it over with fairly quickly, standing up to pedal to maintain his momentum.

"*Caro mio,*" Ned shouted down the hall as Mason came in. "How did it go?"

"Kind of fantastic," Mason yelled back.

Ned walked into the living room and grabbed his forearms, kissing him perfunctorily and looking him over carefully.

"You were worried," Mason said.

"A little, yes. I don't see any stiletto heel marks. You're pretty sweaty, though."

"That would be from cycling home in this heat."

"Was she a total femme fatale?"

"Actually, no. She was kind of ordinary, even affable. And kind of bizarre. She threatened my life, indirectly, but then she bought me lunch. If you take me out to dinner, I'll tell you the whole story."

"Deal," he said. "Mason eats for free all day today. How about that nasty burger joint in West Hollywood that you like? We could celebrate your success."

"You mean the vegan place? That sounds perfectly nasty."

AN HOUR LATER THEY climbed into Ned's Barracuda, and he gingerly backed it out of the garage. Ned loved driving it, but he never drove it like it was a muscle car, showing off its acceleration or speed. "I can't afford to," he'd once said, meaning he didn't want to get cited for recklessness or speeding. It was fun to ride in, nonetheless, with the powerful motor's low rumble.

By the time they'd found a place to park on the street and walked to the restaurant, Mason had told him almost everything about his meeting with Sherri. He left out the connection to the Epworth bankers; even though Ned and Gilbert had helped him make the connection, he had to respect the promise he'd made to Sherri. They got a table and ordered their burgers.

"Tell them to really slather that sauce on for me," Ned instructed the waiter. Then, to Mason, "I'm curious as to whether you were tempted at all, to shake her down for some cash."

"No, because it didn't make sense. If you think about it, I don't actually know enough about her to out her with. I don't know her name or where she lives. The only connection is Champagne, and Sherri knows that. And you know what else? You were right about Champagne. That was totally a wig."

Ned looked at him for a moment. "I'm glad you were able to confirm that."

"And despite her poor fashion choices, I wouldn't want to get her in trouble. So besides enriching myself, there was no point in threatening to out her, only trouble for everyone involved. Along with the threat of winding up in a shallow grave out in the Mojave, of course."

"But you were never even tempted to go for the cash?"

"Would you have been?"

"Maybe. I'm not sure. It would have been interesting to have that option," Ned said.

"I think that's one of the differences between us. You're much more the type of guy who does what you can get away with, and I'm more about doing what's right, whether I can get away with more or not." He wasn't sure whether Ned would be offended or disagree with him, but he just nodded.

"I know you're right. It's like that château in France."

"Exactly," Mason said. They had been walking in the French countryside and come across the driveway to a boarded-up mansion. There were clearly no cars or human activity inside the fence, and there wasn't even a gate across the driveway. Ned had wanted to wander in and poke around, but Mason had refused, pointing out the "Private" sign on the gatepost. "You wouldn't want someone wandering around your yard," he had said.

"I don't think it means I'm immoral," Ned said, "just that I'm more practical, and you're more idealistic. Acting idealistically can't always serve you that well."

"You're right," Mason said. "It doesn't. But it's also my personality. I know myself, and I know I wouldn't be able to sleep at night if I'd taken hush money from her."

"But didn't you want to know more about where the money came from?"

The waiter appeared with their plates, and he'd barely set them down when Ned dove in. "Enjoy," he said, quickly stepping back, as if he were afraid of getting bitten.

"Sure, I'd love to know all about it," Mason said, "but she had no reason to tell me all that. I was shocked that she told me as much as she did. And maybe not knowing everything is somehow better; maybe I'm safer that way. Ultimately, it doesn't matter, because that's not what I was hired to find out."

"The mystery, though. It's like an itch," Ned said through a mouthful of fries. "You seem to be able to let it go more easily than I would. It's such a compelling story."

"I think that's Gilbert's influence. He likes stories about mysterious mysteries, as he calls them, and conspiracies, with grand possibilities but no real solutions. Intrinsically it's compelling because it's something we'll never know."

After they'd eaten, Ned paid the waiter. "Do you want to walk through Boys Town?" he asked Mason. The burger joint was in the straight part of West Hollywood, but the gay part was just a few blocks down the hill.

"Sure. We can walk off the fries."

Despite the heat Ned looped his arm through Mason's as they walked. "I'm glad it went well today," he said. "You've done really well with this new career."

"I can hardly believe it."

"The part that's hard to believe is that it comes

down to psychic power. With all the time you've spent in the library, maybe it's more about regular old research."

"I think it's both. I know you'll probably never believe the psychic thing, I get that. I've heard you. But it seems to be happening nonetheless. And I know you're being as supportive as you can. A truly zealous skeptic never would have gone to a strip club with me."

"I guess I've registered my disbelief clearly enough," Ned said. "I'll try to cut you a little more slack. So what are you going to tell her mother?"

"Well, not the truth."

"Why not?"

"It's too much. How can I tell Miss Cassie that her daughter was a stripper, and traded shoes for blow jobs, and wound up fabulously wealthy? Can you imagine? It sounds like a lie, but even if she believed it … I can't see any benefit in telling her all the sordid details."

"Don't you think she should be able to make that decision for herself?"

"What decision?"

"Well, determining what's sordid and what's not. That's just your perception of it. It's not really your role to edit the truth for other people."

"I guess," Mason said tentatively.

"I just think the truth should trump other considerations. Everything else is inferior."

"Maybe it's about what's constructive and what's not. Maybe telling the whole truth is over-rated. Our parents' generation didn't worry much about it. They wouldn't have been talking about who was a stripper and who dated mobsters."

"Oh, mine might have. At least in private. But if you don't talk about it, that information is gone. I know there were lots of confirmed bachelors and maiden aunts in past generations in my family who were probably gay, and people would have known that back then, even if it wasn't public information. I'd love to know that now, but their stories are lost."

"OK, so I'll write it all down in my notes in the case file, even the part about the blow jobs." They'd reached the boulevard in Boys Town, several blocks of glittering restaurants, bars, and retail stores that saw heavy foot traffic day and night. Mason nodded toward a brightly lit yogurt shop with buff, shirtless young guys working behind the counter. "Was that there before?"

"I've never seen it, no. But if I ate yogurt, that's where I'd go." Ned turned and looked back at someone who had passed them on the sidewalk. "Do you know that guy? He looks so familiar. Is it someone you used to work with?"

"No, but I think I've seen him too. I think he was on TV. I know: it was *Pica Confessions*." They didn't watch much TV, but the few things they did watch were true gems, Mason felt, including perhaps the zenith of the reality genre, *Pica Confessions,* where people who ate things that aren't food were shown repeatedly acting out their compulsion, and then were forced to confess it to a friend or relative.

"Ooh, right," Ned said. "What does he eat?"

"I think he was the person the eater had to

confess to, somebody's dad or brother. Maybe the guy who ate potting soil, or the one who ate dryer sheets."

"I remember that guy. 'Dad, I have something to tell you. I eat dryer sheets.' That's the best celebrity sighting of the year, right there."

"I'll put that in my notes in the case file."

"So there was no discussion with Sherri about having her talk to her mother," Ned said.

"Miss Cassie forbade me from encouraging that. Sherri was aware of that too, that her mother wouldn't want to reconnect. And Sherri certainly didn't want it either."

"But wouldn't it be great if you could help them reconcile?"

"That's totally not my business."

"I wondered if it was the real reason she hired you. Like a passive way to reconnect with her daughter, without having to admit she wanted that."

"I don't think so. She was pretty adamant. I think Mrs. Lewis would be happy to get them back together, but it's no more her business than it is mine."

"Maybe part of the reason Sherri was willing to meet you was a subconscious desire to reconnect with her mother."

"Now you sound like a shrink. I don't think either one of them is especially out of touch with their true desires. I'm pretty sure their schism is the way they both want it. And didn't you just tell me how it's not my place to decide for them what the truth is? It's certainly not my place to interpret their subconscious desires, or worse, to meddle in things they specifically told me to stay out of."

"So no happy endings," he said, and playfully bumped Mason's shoulder with his.

"I think Sherri's happy. She got everything she ever wanted, if you believe her mother. And Miss Cassie seems to have a pretty good life, with a decent job and strong community roots, which is certainly one way to define happiness."

"I guess it is," he said.

"Yo—Braithwaite!" someone shouted from the patio of a crowded pub. They stopped and looked; it was Justine, Mason's former colleague. She pushed her way to the railing at the sidewalk. "Hey, good to see you guys. How are you?"

"I'm well," Mason said. "We just ate, and we're walking it off. We just saw this guy from television. *Pica Confessions.*"

"You look so sedate," she said. "I'd be much more pumped up if I'd just seen someone from *Pica Confessions.* Come in and have a drink with us. I'm here with my cousin Leah for girls' night; you'll love her."

He looked to Ned. "What do you think?"

"Come on, just one," Justine said. "I'm buying."

"You two probably want to talk shop," Ned said. "So we can stop for one. But only on the condition that I'm buying."

They walked around to the entrance and showed the bouncer their IDs. It was less crowded inside, where Justine had returned, and she and

Leah were standing at a tall bar table rather than sitting. Half the people in the place were straight women, Mason thought, based on a cursory glance around, despite the location. She introduced them to Leah, younger than Justine and more dressed up for a night out, complete with a short skirt and long flat-ironed hair that she kept flipping out of her eyes. On top of her head was a small black patch; it was difficult to make out in the dim light, but it must have been a little hat.

"Did you come from a wedding earlier or something?" Mason asked her across the table.

"What?" she shouted over the music, leaning toward him.

"He said he loves your hat," Ned said.

Leah smiled. "Thank you."

Ned flagged down a waiter and ordered drinks.

"Why do you come to Boys Town for girls' night?" Mason asked Justine, leaning close to her to be heard over the music.

"So that we focus less on guys," she shouted back, though Mason saw that Leah had taken an immediate animated interest in chatting with Ned.

"Does she know he's gay?" Mason asked her.

Justine laughed. "You don't have to worry about Leah."

Their round arrived, and Ned paid the waiter. "I love that you two are drinking beer," he said. "It's cheaper than cocktails." He had ordered Mason a beer too, and a tonic water for himself.

"That's no fun," Leah said, clinking her glass on his.

"I'm driving," he said with a shrug. It was easier than explaining that he was in recovery, which, Mason knew, inevitably led to questions about the minutiae of his addiction and sobriety.

Leah chatted with Ned, and Justine leaned close to Mason and launched into a diatribe about his former employers, to which he mostly nodded in response. Emotionally she was still right there, still caught up in the drama, which made him realize that he was actually free of it now. So much had happened since then. And he had been so ready to move on that he was able to put it behind him fairly quickly.

Someone passed them a clipboard with a karaoke sign-up sheet and a booklet with a list of the available songs.

"That may be our cue to leave," Mason said, even though he still had half a beer in hand.

"Oh, Mason, you should sing," Leah said. "You're tall, like Dean Martin. I bet you sound great. Do a Rat Pack song."

"No way," he said, shaking his head.

"How do you know who Dean Martin is?" Justine said. "I'm older than you, and I barely know who he is."

Ned said, "Mason's right. He sounds like a cat caught in a vacuum cleaner when he tries to sing."

"Oh!"

"Well, maybe some type of large red-furred vegan mammal," Ned clarified, "but still, caught in a vacuum."

"OK, then," Mason said, and took the clip-

board. There were only a couple of names on the
sheet, so in the third position he wrote "Ned Vélez"
in large print, carefully adding the accent over the
e to ensure complete accuracy. He flipped through
the booklet and picked the most appropriate song
he could find—Tammy Wynette's "Stand by Your
Man"—and wrote the code for it beside Ned's name.

The bar didn't really have a stage, but there was
a little floor space at the back where the karaoke
machine and mike stand were set up. The first two
performers walked up readily when their names
were called, and they both did awkward renditions
of songs that must have been current pop hits.
When Ned's name was called, he didn't respond,
but Justine laughed and realized what Mason had
done, and started pointing at Ned.

"Ned Vélez?" the host said again into the mike.

"Over here," Justine shouted. "Don't be shy,
Nedly."

He figured out what was happening and managed to mouth "You brat" to Mason, as Leah and
Justine pushed him toward the mike and people in
the bar started to chant "Ned, Ned, Ned." He was
swept to the karaoke machine, and the mike was
shoved into his hand.

The introductory bars of the song were playing, and when he looked at the lyrics on the screen,
he visibly winced. But when the verse started, he
sang the words, using the same Southern twang as
Tammy had in her original. "Sometimes it's hard
to be a woman / Giving all your love to just one
man ..."

Justine and Leah whooped, and a few others laughed and clapped. He glared at Mason when he sang the lyric "But if you love him, you'll forgive him," and by the time he reached the chorus, half the bar was singing with him. He ended the song to much applause, with a flourish and a bow worthy of a Shakespearean performance, and then slunk back to their table.

"What a good sport," Leah said.

"I guess I deserved that," he said. "But I stand by my earlier comments, if not always by my man."

"I'm not denying what you said about my dearth of musical talent, but I thought you might be able to do better yourself," Mason said.

Not too much later, when he had had enough of Justine's emotional job trauma and the karaoke was really getting irritating, Mason told them he and Ned had to go. They air-kissed Justine and Leah good-bye and walked out onto the cool, quiet sidewalk.

"I haven't laughed like that in weeks," Ned said as they made their way back to the car.

"You did pretty well, considering you didn't rehearse," Mason said.

Ned put his arm around his waist and said, "Well, thanks for picking a song that wasn't beyond my vocal range."

As Mason climbed into the Barracuda and got comfortable, he realized he was really tired. "Maybe *Metro Grooves* is still on," he said, and clicked on the radio. It was, but he left the volume fairly low. Ned looked tired too. They rode in comfortable silence, and Ned put his hand on top of Mason's.

As they waited at a traffic light on a back street in East Hollywood, a woman pushing a shopping cart stepped slowly into the crosswalk in front of them. It was still warm out, but she was wearing a woolen hat and a heavy winter coat over pink sweatpants. When she was halfway across the street, she turned and walked back to the sidewalk, leaving the cart where it was. In the dark Mason hadn't noticed that there were four more carts. She started to push the second one across. The light turned green.

"This might take a while," he said.

"I think that's the Comet woman," Ned said. "See the white powder all over her coat and the shopping carts? That's Comet."

"How do you know that?"

"She's around here all the time. Have you ever noticed big patches of white powder on the sidewalk around here? That's from her. Apparently she dry-bathes in the Comet."

"Doesn't that stuff have bleach in it? She really shouldn't do that."

He looked over at Mason. "I think she might have more pressing issues than skin care, don't you?"

"I don't know; bleach is pretty bad. It makes the protein molecules in your skin unfold and clump together. And you know how bleach feels slippery? That's because it's turning the oils in your skin into soap. It causes irreversible damage."

"Well, hopefully she reads *Scientific American* so she'll realize how harmful it is."

"Are you sure it's Comet?"

"Gilbert saw her one time bathing with a can of it. He talked to her, and she said she found cases of it in a Dumpster behind a drug store. I think that's mostly what's in all her shopping carts."

Sure enough, it looked like at least some of the carts were piled up with green cans of cleanser. Mason watched her walk slowly back to the curb and marshal another cart.

Suddenly something clicked in his head. "Oh, wow … I know who Peggy's father is," he said.

"What?"

"I just figured it out."

"From watching the Comet woman?" Ned asked.

"No. I mean, yes, sort of."

"So who is he?"

"He was a guitarist at the Helios nightclub in the eighties."

"How could you possibly know that?"

"I don't know. But I know. I think I had a psychic flash," he said. "My mind was wandering, you know, Comet, actual comets, space, Gilbert's damn aliens, space again, the sun, *sol,* Helios, the Helios nightclub. But it was more than that. I think I know what he looks like. I kind of got an image."

"Did you get a name?"

"No. I'm going to have to do some research, but I'm sure I can find him."

"Maybe you shouldn't mention it to her until you're sure."

"I am sure. And why not?"

"If you give her false hope, it'll kill her. I'm just saying, think carefully about what you're doing."

More skepticism, Mason thought. But he wasn't going to get into it now. This insight was way too important.

The Comet woman had dragged her last cart safely across the road. The traffic light had cycled through several times, and just before it turned green again, she turned to look into the car at them. Her face folded into a crooked gap-toothed smile, and she nodded. Mason was still hyperattuned after his flash of insight, and he wondered if the Comet woman had had something to do with it. If he went all the way down the psychic rabbit hole, he thought, maybe he would wind up like her. Maybe she was the most enlightened person in the city. Maybe she had perfect clarity and unlimited insight beyond the boundaries of the world everyone else saw, and she had simply renounced all the trappings of it to focus on pure awareness. Maybe she had shared something with him in that moment as they waited for her to cross the road. Maybe she was a gifted sage who only appeared insane and bedraggled because no one accepted the validity of what she could do. Maybe the shopping carts were a performance, or a symbol just for him, or a medium, like the Ouija board or a deck of tarot cards.

Ned eased the Barracuda through the intersection.

Mostly to himself, Mason said, "I think my mind has officially just been blown."

Peggy was still up when they came in. She was sitting at the dining table with stacks of paperwork, presumably more of her mother's stuff.

"Hey, Margaret," Ned greeted her. "You didn't play tonight?"

"Don't call me that, or I'll start calling you Eddie. And no, I didn't, not until Saturday." Ned chuckled and went down the hall to change, and she asked Mason, "How was the meeting with the mystery woman? You're still alive, I see. That's a good sign."

"It was pretty great. She's not at all what I expected."

"It was really the shrink's daughter?"

"Yeah, it was her." Mason sat down at the table with her and told her about meeting Sherri, and how she had reinvented herself, omitting the part about Mickey Burke. He explained the version of the truth he planned to take back to Miss Cassie.

"She'll be satisfied that you did the work, even if you're not going to tell her the details," she said.

"Peggy, something else happened tonight. I think I got a bit of psychic insight about your father."

"Really?" she said, looking dubious. "What kind of insight?"

"Well, I think I saw him. And I'm pretty sure I can find out more about him, but it'll take me a day or two. I don't have a name or anything, not yet."

"You saw him in your mind?" she asked.

Mason nodded.

"What did he look like?"

"He had blond hair, kind of dirty blond, and a round face. He looked kind of thick: not overweight, but like a football player's build. His facial features looked like yours."

"When did this happen?" She sank back in her chair.

"I honestly think the information has been there for a while, kind of floating in my subconscious, but it clicked into my waking mind just now, on the way home. We were waiting for the Comet woman to cross the street."

"Oh, I've seen her. That does take a while."

"How come I'm the only one who doesn't know about the Comet woman?"

"It's probably because you're on your bicycle. You don't have to wait for her; you can just go around."

"Ah."

"Listen, Mason, about my dad. I hope this is real. Don't break my heart." Her eyes had teared up.

"I'll try not to," he said. "I know this is important, and I wouldn't mislead you. I wouldn't have told you about it if it wasn't a solid lead."

"I'm going to call Helen tomorrow and see if your description reminds her of anyone. As soon as you find out anything, or get any other psychic insights, you'll let me know?"

"You'll know as soon as I do."

MASON WAS COMPLETELY EXHAUSTED but still exhilarated from his breakthrough when he and

Ned went to bed, and he decided he couldn't go to sleep without connecting with his inner senses. One idea among psychic theorists, he had read, is that inspiration is a connection with the broader reality, which people don't tune in to with their conscious minds. In the dream world everyone has access to all parts of reality, and inspiration in the waking world is a transfer of some of that information when it's needed or useful. He suspected that his flash of inspiration might have been just that, bleed-through from the dream world, perhaps courtesy of the Comet woman, perhaps not.

Ned was already asleep, he realized, and he put his arm across his belly and slid close to him. Even at that late hour it was still so warm that he knew it would only last a few minutes until they both sought cooler air and pulled apart, but it was worth it even for a moment. As he drifted off, in the hypnagogic state he gave himself the suggestion that he'd connect with some other part of himself that had more information about Peggy's father.

He dreamed about people, but he didn't really think he was connecting with anything significant. At one point he was talking to a Roman soldier who was wearing an imperial bronze helmet complete with muttonchop side guards. The man had an intense, vacant look in his eyes, and Mason was afraid of him, but there he stood, too afraid to move away. Later he was sitting on the deck of a public swimming pool, watching a woman lead a swimming class. She looked to be at least in her sixties and had short hair. She stood at the side of the pool, gently cajoling her students. She seemed friendly, but Mason wasn't even interacting with her; he was just sitting on the other side of the pool. He wasn't able to become aware that he was dreaming, and eventually drifted into dreamlessness.

Saturday

PEGGY WAS GONE AND Ned was immersed in his work when Mason got up in the morning, after eleven, embarrassingly late even for him. He made it through his first pot of coffee and felt awake enough to call Miss Cassie.

"Mason," she said when he identified himself. "I was thinking about you this morning."

"I have some news for you," he said.

"I suppose that was inevitable. I have some money for you, and some updates. Can you swing by my office today?"

"Sure, maybe a bit later in the afternoon? I'm in the middle of some stuff, and I have a couple of other stops to make."

"I plan to be here until nine o'clock tonight, so any time is fine. I only have a couple of clients scheduled."

She must not have an especially active social life, he thought, if she was working until nine on a Saturday night.

He rode down the hill and locked up his bike at the metro station before heading downtown. His errands were all within a few blocks of Miss Cassie's office, so he wouldn't need his wheels.

His first stop was a print shop, a small storefront in the financial district. He was happy that the door was open when he pulled on it, considering it was Saturday. Downtown was changing, with more residential space opening up, which meant shops expanding their business hours to the weekend. There was no one inside except the clerk, a young guy with wavy long hair and full-sleeve tattoos. He stood up from his desk when Mason walked in.

"Can I help you?" he asked.

"I need some business cards."

"My specialty."

"I have a graphic that I can send you," Mason said, pulling out his phone. "And I'll write down what the text part should be. What's your email?" He typed it into his phone with his thumbs as the clerk recited it. "I'm thinking the graphic should be on the left, and the text on the right, in a fairly ordinary typeface. Everything in plain black and white."

"Let me pull it up." The clerk slid a pad of paper

and a pencil along the counter to Mason, and then leaned over his computer. A moment later he said, "Oh … kay … do you mean this?" He turned the screen toward Mason, and there was Peggy's illustration in all its glory.

"Yes, that's it. It's amazing, right? My friend did that. She's very talented."

"Uh, sure, if you say so." He turned the screen back. "Is that even the right way up?"

"Yes, that's right. And here's the text. I'm sure you'll be able to balance everything nicely." He twisted the pad around so the clerk could read it.

"Mason Braithwaite, Psychic Investigations." He looked up at him. "Maybe that image is more appropriate than I thought. So just the phone number and email address?"

"Right."

"I guess people can always get your other details psychically."

He wasn't smiling, so Mason didn't know whether he was making a joke, but he laughed anyway. "And can you put a tiny black pinstripe between my name and 'Psychic Investigations' below it?"

"Of course." He picked up the pen and made a note on the pad. "How many cards do you need?"

"I guess a thousand, to get started."

"I'll send you a sample at your email address in a day or two, and we can go from there."

Mason walked back to Fifth Street and into the central library. He headed down to the history department, at the building's very lowest sublevel, symbolically the foundation of everything else.

Librarians, he had found, are almost universally patient. It probably becomes a necessity, after being asked the same questions hundreds of times a day. A librarian had once confided to him that she was just happy when patrons weren't homeless, because the homeless were usually malodorous. When enough of them were in her department, she said, the air became so rank that she got a migraine. Today the air down in this part of the building seemed reasonably clear, and the young woman who helped him out had a ready smile. She also had her hair in a bun and wore glasses with thick black frames and round lenses, a living and breathing stereotype of a librarian from 1928. He considered mentioning this, but kept it to himself.

"I want to look at city newspapers from the early 1980s," he said, "but I don't even know what papers existed back then. I know they're probably not in the electronic newspaper database."

"No, they're not. Everything from that era is microfilm. I have an index of the newspapers we have," she said, and pulled out the document.

"Which one of these would be best for arts listings?" Mason asked.

"Well, you could start with the *Los Angeles Daily Bugle*. It's defunct, but back then it had a pretty extensive calendar section."

He requested a couple of months' worth of microfilm copies for 1983, which she brought to him at the microfilm readers. They were positioned in a dark corner, presumably to make it easier to read the backlit viewing screens, and he hunkered down in front of one. It took a few minutes to get used to the machine's controls, but soon he was zooming through pages of decades-old news. The librarian had been right—the *Bugle*'s entertainment section was useful; there were extensive club listings, including for Helios. The club appeared regularly, and scanning through a couple of months of weekend listings, he figured out that it had a house band, Warren and the Rabbits, that played whenever there wasn't a headline act. He went back to the librarian and asked if the newspapers were indexed in any way.

"Sure they are. You'll have to use our computer. Just grab a seat at that terminal, and I'll get you set up," she said. She got him connected to the correct database and left him alone.

There were six entries for Warren and the Rabbits, all dating to 1983 and 1984 except for one in 1991. He already had a couple of the corresponding spools, and he requested the others. The first entry he found was a puff piece on the band when it was new and had just started playing at Helios. It described the kind of music they played, which sounded a lot like what Mason would call lounge music; the band even had a xylophonist, the eponymous Warren. He rewound the spool, loaded another, and zoomed through to the second entry, a short article and a photo. He felt a surge of excitement as he twisted a knob on the machine to get the photo into sharper focus. This was it. The photo showed the band with their instruments, all five of them smiling for the camera, Warren with his xylophone mallets poised above the instrument's bars. They were dressed casually, in denim and the wide collars of the era. The photograph had been taken from a lower level, looking slightly up at them.

And there he was. The guy Mason had seen in his flash of insight. He was sitting on a stool on the left side of the photo, cradling an electric guitar. He looked exactly the same, with longish hair, a moon-shaped face, and a thick build. Even in black-and-white, with the newsprint grain, Mason could tell he was blond. And there was no doubt that this was Peggy's father: he looked just like her. Even though he was heavier and she was wiry like her mother had been, his eyes and the shape of his nose were hers. The resemblance was remarkable.

He had done it: he had found Peggy's dad for her. Maybe this could help her transform her longing, and help her work through the grief of losing her mother.

He pressed the button labeled "Print" so that he could take a copy to show Peggy. Somewhere near the librarians' counter he heard a printer quietly come to life. He pulled his notepad out of his backpack and wrote down the page number and date so that she could find it herself later if she wanted to.

He read the article accompanying the photo. It was mostly about renovations at the nightclub, but it included the band members' names; Peggy's father was listed as "George Martin, guitars." It didn't sound like a stage name, and Mason thought he might be able to dig up something more on him. He checked the other articles listed for the band, the pages zooming by on the screen until he found the right issue, then crawling by until he found the right headline. He didn't find any more photos, but the 1991 article was a shock: a short obituary for George Martin, styled as a news item. It didn't say how he had died, but charitable donations were to be made to the California Heart Disease Foundation. He remembered the image of a throbbing heart he'd had when he read the deposit pouch at St. Agatha's. Could that image have been connected to Peggy's dad?

The obit said that he'd left behind a grieving widow and a son. Damn, Peggy had a half brother. That is going to blow her mind, he thought. George had been the "longtime guitarist in the club band Warren and the Rabbits" and had "performed on many film scores." With the details in this item, it would be easy to find Peggy's biological half brother, and maybe even her dad's widow, or his bandmates. Mason pressed "Print" again, and then rewound the spool and zipped his notepad back into his backpack. He'd leave the rest of the research to her; he had done enough to get things started. He thought of harvesting bamboo shoots, which he'd done once in Northern California. It was a skill in itself just to find the tiny bump in the earth where the shoot was preparing to protrude. If its tiny leaves were already visible, it was too old to be harvested. So one person would locate the shoot using only sight, and someone else would do the grunt work of digging it out of the earth. He had located the bump in the earth for Peggy, and now she could take on the work of finding her father's friends and relatives.

He handed all the boxes of microfilm back to the librarian at the counter, collected his printouts, and paid her for them.

"You found everything you needed?" she asked.

"Much more than I expected. You've been most helpful."

"Of course," she said, beaming at him over her antique glasses.

Walking out onto the street, he realized he'd been in the bowels of the library for a long time; the shadows of the office towers had grown long as the sun approached the horizon. Waiting at a street corner for the crossing signal, he texted Ned and Peggy that he wouldn't be home for dinner.

The Primavera Building was just a couple of blocks away. Walking toward it, he got a different perspective than when he'd come up out of the metro the other day—of the side that faced away from the street. It was plain painted brick with a few small ventilating windows, obviously designed to be hidden by a building of similar height next door. But the space next door was now a surface parking lot, exposing the plain wall as much as the facade. What we see on closer inspection isn't always the most attractive part, he thought. Still, he ogled the art deco facade from the street and the murals in the lobby as he waited for the elevator; it was like time-traveling, from the 1930s street-side view up to Miss Cassie's decidedly twenty-first-century office.

The sign on her office door said "Come in." Miss Cassie was seated at her desk, peering at her computer screen. She didn't look up, but held up her index finger in a "wait a minute" gesture. Mason stood awkwardly in the office's entryway and looked out the tall windows that ran the length of the office, to the parking lot below and the office towers of the financial district beyond. He turned to look at a framed black-and-white photograph on the wall next to him. It showed a row of desks lined up along the same windows. Several office workers sat at the desks or stood nearby, and a massive flower arrangement perched on a credenza. The men sitting at the desks could have been from any one of several long-ago decades, with their snug suits and close-cropped hair, but the women gave it away as the 1930s, with their tight permanent-wave curls and dowdy floral-print dresses. He looked back to Miss Cassie's windows; this was definitely the same office as in the old photo, or at least the same set of windows, possibly on another floor. The image looked familiar, he realized, and then it struck him; he'd seen it when he had done psychometry on the safe at St. Agatha's.

"Mason," Miss Cassie said finally, standing up from her desk. "Sorry to keep you waiting. Always a pleasure." He saw that along with her dark skirt and jacket, she had a colorful scarf tied loosely around her neck. The pattern printed on it was birds of paradise, like the dress Sherri had been wearing when he met her. What were the odds?

Mason took a deep breath to calm himself. "Miss Cassie, what's this photo? I've seen it before."

"It was taken in this very building, when it opened in 1931. It was an insurance company office then, and the flowers are there because they had just moved in. I thought it was interesting to see what it looked like all those years ago. Look at the windows, though. They're the same as mine. That's the only part that still looks the same."

"Yes, they do. But I saw this image when I was at St. Agatha's last week."

"No, you couldn't have. The only copy I have of that photo is here."

"I saw it in a psychic vision when I did a reading on the safe in the office at St. Agatha's. Remember when I did that?"

"I remember," she said. "But how do you know it's the same thing?"

"It was very vivid. I remember the row of desks and the flowers in the same configuration. Miss Cassie, I think that safe might have been here in this office back then. It's certainly old enough."

"Come and sit down," she said, and walked around her desk to sit in one of the chairs in the sitting area. Mason sat on the sofa facing her.

"It goes way beyond a coincidence," he said. "It demonstrates that the universe has intricate inter-connections that we're usually unaware of." The safe, the birds of paradise on her scarf and Sherri's outfit, the beating heart—it felt like he was suddenly seeing the links that run through the world unnoticed.

"The safe does have a connection to this office, but it's no coincidence. They were gutting another floor of this building a few years ago and were going to sell it for scrap. I claimed it and took it to St. Agatha's. It's so heavy, it cost me a fortune to have it moved. You must have made the connection when you saw that photo from the same era."

"But I had the vision of the office before I saw the photo."

"Or did you see the office in the photo when you came here," she said, "and then backfill the story about reading the safe? I'm not saying you did it willfully, just that the subconscious mind works in mysterious ways."

"I know what I saw, and I'm not backfilling. I'm not sure now what the vision means, if it means anything, but maybe there's a meaningful connec-tion between you and that safe."

"In that case, I'll have to have a closer look at it next time I'm over there," she said, raising her eyebrows.

"That's a great idea. And when you look at it, focus on the symbolism, like what it means for you, or what associations it has for you, or what feelings come up."

"Now it sounds like you're straying into my field. What about you? What kind of feelings do you have from recognizing the photo?"

"Uh, I guess it makes me happy. You might think I'm backfilling, but I know it was real, and it means I really can do this psychic thing, picking up images and connections beyond the five senses."

"And that feeling gives you confidence in your work."

"Yes, it does," Mason said, but he wondered, What the hell was she talking about? He'd solved her missing money mystery; why did she care whether he had confidence in his work or not?

"OK." She nodded slowly, watching him, but didn't say anything.

"So, then, what's the news from the police about your missing collection steward? I think you mentioned that on the phone," Mason said, diverting the conversation from her uncomfortable silence. "Did they find him?"

"He's still in the wind, as they say, but there is news. I had given his personnel file to the detective, with his photo and everything he had told us about himself. It turns out the photo didn't match the name and Social Security number, or anything else."

"Identity theft?" Mason said.

"Exactly. It turns out the real Michael moved to Atlanta, where he's a reasonably upstanding citizen. That's why we got such good recommendations from his church in San Diego. They thought they were recommending someone else."

"Clever. So who is the guy?"

"Using the photo, the police were able to find out. He's a punk with a rap sheet as long as your arm, coincidentally also named Michael." She shook her head, and Mason could see her anger wasn't far beneath the surface. "And take a guess as to what he learned to do in state prison during his last stint."

"Uh, making license plates?"

"Close. He studied metalworking."

"Oh," he said slowly. "So he built the metal plate with the hidden compartment himself."

"Probably. I'm not thrilled that we're paying to enable people like that to reoffend more effectively, but the detective figures that he'll go away for a long time this time. Besides burglary and grand theft, they searched his apartment and found some of the checks stolen from St. Agatha's, including some that were being soaked to take the ink off them. So that's fraud. And there was a fake Social Security card, which apparently is one of the most serious charges."

"Why would he be soaking the ink off the checks?"

"Well, then you can write in your own name as the payee, and whatever amount you want. The detective said he was likely too smart to try cashing them himself, so he was probably selling them to other lowlifes."

"And why would he leave that stuff lying around his apartment?"

"They think he never went back there after we scared him away on Sunday. He left town. The police say he has contacts out of state, so they're following up on that."

"I hope they catch him."

"They will. It's only a matter of time. The long arm of the law, and all that." She sat back in her chair and sighed. "So, on another unsavory topic, you suggested that you found out something about Sherri?"

"Yes," he said. "I was able to speak to her briefly. She's fine."

"On the phone, or in person? Where is she living?"

"In person."

"So she's here in town. What's she doing? And what name is she using?"

"I can't say, because I don't know. But I did see her, and she assured me that everything is going well in her life."

"That must mean she struck it rich," she said.

"I think you might be right about that. She was dressed quite nicely."

"But you didn't even get her new name? How did you find her?"

"I can't actually tell you that, because my sources requested anonymity. I have to respect that."

"An interesting moral stance for a psychic," she said, and stared at him for a moment. "How do I know you're not making it all up so you can fleece us?"

Mason felt his cheeks redden. "That's a fair question. I know it must sound like a lie. Who would go meet a missing person and not find out anything about her new life, right? But you know her, and you know she wanted to change things when she left you. Part of that is maintaining her privacy, and her condition for meeting me was that I stick to that. And as you requested, I didn't suggest that she get in touch with you either; she didn't even believe I was working for you until I told her Mrs. Lewis was the one who actually hired me." He thought for a moment. "Here's something she told me that nobody else would have known: when she was an adolescent, you made her cry for thirty minutes a day to release her repressed anger or something, and you stood there and watched her to make sure she did it."

Her face clouded with anger. "You don't know anything about it." She struggled to regain her composure, looking out the windows for a moment. "You're right, though. Nobody else would have known about that."

"I'm sorry if I've upset you."

"You haven't. But I guess that means I believe you." She rubbed her eyes with her fingers, and when she pulled them away, she looked tired. She said, "Was she happy, at least?"

"I think so. I don't know what she was like

before, but she seemed happy, yes. I think she really does have a good life now."

Miss Cassie nodded, looking at the floor and seeming lost in thought.

"I guess I'll call Mrs. Lewis tomorrow," Mason said, "and let her know what I found out, and maybe discuss whether she's willing to pay me, considering the lack of detail."

"No, no. You let me deal with Betty. I'll pay you, even though she's the one who offered."

"Well, she gave me lemonade and cookies. I feel like I should at least call her."

"Wait—cookies that she made?"

"I have no idea. I didn't try them."

"Consider yourself lucky. I've never had the heart to tell her, but that woman cannot cook. I think it's why her husband worked so hard all those years, so that they could afford to eat out more. Anyway, call her if you want, but she's going to have a lot of questions. I know how to handle her. If I were you, I'd leave it to me." She stood up and smoothed the front of her skirt. "Let me get some cash from my safe; sit tight." She walked around toward the doorway in the only internal wall in the office, but stopped and turned back. "Listen, don't get me wrong; I'm not ungrateful. I appreciate you doing the work, and I'm surprised you were able to find her. In some way I'm glad to know she's doing all right."

Maybe I will get paid, Mason thought. He could understand her being dubious about his story, and he wouldn't have blamed her for not wanting to pay him at all.

She reappeared a moment later from the back room with two envelopes in hand. "This is for unmasking our thief," she said, "and this one is for finding Sherri."

"Thank you," he said, standing to take the envelopes. He started to unzip his backpack to tuck them inside.

"Wait a minute. You have to count it. I want you to fill out a receipt; I'm going to deduct it as a business expense."

"OK," Mason said, and flipped open the un-sealed flap of the first envelope. "Jesus, are these hundreds?" He looked at her in shock. "There must be three grand in here."

"Forty-two hundred," she said.

"But we agreed on two hundred bucks."

"Yes, your fee is in there, plus two thousand as a bonus for figuring out who the thief was. You saved us at least that much, and probably a lot more. The other two thousand is a bonus for the stolen prop-erty recovered in Michael's apartment. If all those checks had been circulated, it would have cost a dozen different people far more than that. I said there would be a bonus for you if we got an arrest, and there's an arrest warrant, which is just as good for my purposes."

"But it seems excessive."

"No, it isn't. Another way to look at it is that we're paying the rate you originally requested, remember that? Five hundred a day plus expenses. I balked at the time, but in hindsight it seems more reasonable. We appreciate your hard work. And rather than arguing about it, why not just accept that you've earned it?"

"OK." He nodded. He could do that. He riffled through the bills quickly, pretending to count them.

"There's another four thousand in the other envelope for finding Sherri. I'm sure it was at least that much work, even if it didn't take eight days. And you did exactly as I asked, not bringing her around here, not staging a reunion. It comes with a condition, though."

"Miss Cassie, that's incredibly generous, thank you. What's the condition?"

"That I don't have to hear about it anymore. You did the work, and despite the inevitable ten thousand questions she'll have, Betty will be satisfied. Anyway, the point is, now we can let sleeping dogs lie."

"Fine by me." It struck him that part of the reason she paid him a premium was for not giving her any details about Sherri. It's what she had wanted all along, not to deal with it, but to have a framework for that. Maybe he had sensed from the beginning that the best result of his inquiries for Miss Cassie would be an extremely abbreviated version of the truth, and in that way he had done exactly what she'd asked.

"One last question, though. When you read her necklace, you got the image of a green diamond, or something like that. What did that mean?"

"I never found out," he lied.

"So it's just like the collection plates. You can't really claim to have used psychic abilities to find her."

"Yes and no. It also took a lot of real-world legwork."

"And that was all here in the city?" she said, raising her eyebrows.

"Miss Cassie, you just finished telling me that you didn't want to know any more about it."

"I did, didn't I." She smiled. "I guess if I were to be completely honest, I'd have to admit I want it both ways. We wouldn't be human without our contradictions, as we say in my business."

"I guess I should go," Mason said, tucking the cash envelopes into his backpack.

"Are you in a rush to get somewhere?"

"No, not really."

"Then sit down for a minute. I have a client coming in a little while, but until then we can finish this up."

He sat, and she went to her desk, where she pulled her receipt booklet from a drawer. She passed it to him with a pen, and sat down again across from him. She had also picked up her tablet, he noticed.

"Your name and Social Security number are the important parts," she said, "as well as your mailing address. And I'll warn you now: I'm going to 1099 you in January."

"Of course," he said. "That goes without saying." He filled out the form and then pulled his notepad out of his backpack; he wrote "1099 in

January?" on it so that he'd remember to ask Ned what that meant.

When he had passed the booklet back to her, she said, "Now. How strongly do you believe in this psychic ability of yours?"

"Uh … I guess I believe it more every day. I'm getting better at it, seeing more connections, and hopefully getting more accurate. But you still don't believe it? I accomplished everything that you wanted me to do."

"I believe some people have psychic abilities, but I don't know if I've seen anything to show that that includes you."

"Did I not just solve two mysteries for you using my psychic abilities? You must have approved of my methods, if I'm walking out of here with eight grand." He could feel the color rising in his cheeks, but he wanted to remain calm with her.

"Eighty-two hundred," she corrected, looking at the receipt booklet in her hand, then setting it on the sofa beside her. "And I don't mean to provoke you, but I'm curious about what's at the root of this. Most people who come to see me either have trouble containing their emotions, or they have their emotions so bottled up that they start to be expressed in unpredictable ways."

"I didn't come to see you."

"But in a way, you have." She smiled. "Who was your primary caregiver when you were a child?"

"Uh, I guess my mother."

"What kind of parent was she?"

"My mother? Well, in a word, I'd have to say

inconsistent. I was never sure where I stood. I think it still affects me to this day with things like self-confidence."

She nodded thoughtfully. "Was there another parent?"

"My dad," Mason said. This is crazy, he thought, and frustrating, and certainly none of her business. But she had just paid him more money than he'd seen in one place in years, and there seemed little harm in indulging her for a few minutes.

"And what kind of parent was he?"

"More consistent than my mother. He got sober when I was eight, so before that he was a bit absent, and afterward I remember life was much better."

"Uh-huh." She detached the stylus from her tablet and began writing on it. "He had been an alcoholic?"

"Yes."

"Siblings?"

"A brother, older, and a sister, younger."

"So you were the middle child."

"Indeed I was."

"And you're partnered now?"

"Yes. His name is Ned."

"Would you say that Ned is supportive of you?"

"Very much so."

"So he believes you have the psychic power, and he thinks it's reasonable for you to be making your living this way."

"Well, no, he doesn't believe it at all. He's a non-theist, so he doesn't believe in anything religious, or paranormal, or unscientific. Although I think he believes in aliens, which doesn't seem very scientific. But he's basically supportive of me doing this as a career. He's a twelve-stepper too, like my dad, so he's able to let me do my thing without interfering too much." He had a sudden thought. "Oh, god."

"What is it?" she asked.

"Nothing."

"It's not nothing. You just thought of something." She looked at him expectantly; clearly she wasn't going to let it go.

"Well, I just realized that I kind of married my dad."

"Lots of people do," she said simply. "That's not strange at all. The important thing is whether it's working or not. Have you thought about what your life would look like without Ned in it?"

"I remember what it was like," he said. "We've only been together about three years. It's definitely better with him in it."

"So you said there's alcoholism in your family," she said, scrawling more notes on her tablet. She looked up to ask, "Have you had that kind of problem yourself?"

"I don't think so, no. I drink, but only once in a while, and only one or two. I suppose I'm wary of it becoming a problem because of my dad."

"Drugs?"

"Me? No. Ibuprofen, sometimes, if that counts, and lots of caffeine. Miss Cassie, what's with all the questions?"

She looked up from her tablet. "Well, you did

some work for me, so I thought I could do some work for you."

"Like psychotherapy? Do you think I need that?"

"You do have some deep-seated, uh, alternative ideas about how the world works. And I think everyone can benefit from talking to an objective outsider."

"Actually, Ned said something like that recently too."

"So you're not opposed to the idea."

"Well … no … I guess not. But I wasn't really expecting—"

"Listen, Mason," she said, standing up and walking back to her desk. "I think you're already making progress, and we've only just begun. But I have another appointment coming up here very soon. Can we take this up again next week? Let's say Friday.…" She peered at her desktop screen. "I know you're not a morning person, so how about four o'clock?"

"Uh, OK." He quickly scribbled the day and time on his notepad and stood up.

"On your way out, could you slide the little sign on my door over so that it says 'Please knock'? Thanks. See you Friday."

"OK, then," Mason said, and headed for the door. "Good-bye."

What a weird day, he thought as he rode down the elevator. She had basically bamboozled him into becoming her client. He could blow her off, of course, but maybe it wouldn't hurt to have a little head-shrinking done. He wondered if she was any good at it.

He'd deal with it later, though, as there was still so much to do. So much to tell Peggy, and so much to tell Ned. Despite all the naysaying and disbelief, he had 8,200 validations of his skills sitting in his backpack. He needed to get better at it, he knew—more confident, and less fearful about the process and the people he dealt with. But for the first time in years he felt like he was in charge of things, and was determining his own path forward, and it seemed like the universe was sending him nothing but confirmation that this was the right thing. He stepped out into the fresh air and walked toward the metro entrance, looking up at the soaring architecture all around. It was finally starting to cool off. What a beautiful evening.